M000012347

MY FATHER'S INDIAN

MY FATHER'S INDIAN

How a Butterfly Split the Oak

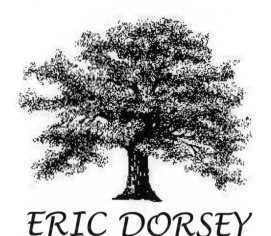

ERIC DORSEY

Copyright © 2020 Eric Dorsey

All rights reserved.

No part of this publication may be reproduced, distributed, or transmitted in any form or by any means, including photocopying, recording, or other electronic or mechanical methods, without the prior written permission of the copyright owner, except in the case of brief quotations embodied in critical reviews and certain other noncommercial uses permitted by copyright law.

ISBN-13: 978-0-578-81034-8 (Paperback Edition)

My Father's Indian: How a Butterfly Split the Oak is a work of fiction. Names, characters, places, and incidents are either products of the author's imagination or are used fictitiously. Any resemblance to actual persons, living or dead, events or locales is entirely coincidental.

"Hidden Ocean", by Brian Andreas, printed with permission
Excerpt from "Inevitable Ecstasy", Session Four,
by Alan Watts, printed with permission

Front cover art by Eric Dorsey
Back cover photograph by Eric Dorsey
Interior design by Eric Dorsey

Printed and bound in the United States of America
First paperback edition November 2020
Cabin View Publishing

For Leigh

Who kept me sane in our teens
And began my search for connection
In the kindest way possible

Contents

PROLOGUE

Time is the substance from which I am made.
Time is a river which carries me along, but I am the river;
It is a tiger that devours me, but I am the tiger;
It is a fire that consumes me, but I am the fire.

Jorge Luis Borges

Slowly, gently, I begin to dance.

Eyes closed, swaying before the bedroom mirror, I struggle to recapture the feeling. A weakness, this indulgence. Pausing, I peek at my reflection. We stare in silence, but after a moment she offers the slightest nod. Right. Today I need it, and that's ok.

A deep measured breath, inhale through the nose, exhale through the mouth. Once, twice, three times, relax, release. And I'm able to let go, sliding back in time, committed to a self-soothing habit dating back to my teens.

Three children, nine years old. Early autumn. The lightly sloping field, the gurgle of the creek, my sundress ruffling against downy legs with a cool breeze. How did that feel exactly?

I close my eyes tighter, dragging the tips of my shoes along the floor as I dance, channeling the long past warmth and grit of bare feet on sunbaked dirt. The vision of those ever-filthy feet makes me smile. Taking another deep breath, I pause momentarily, pressing one shoe flat against the wood floor, willing my adult foot to feel soft dirt lightly giving, shifting, squeezing between my tiny nine-year-old toes.

A beat passes, longer than usual. I relax, dismiss the fear, focus. Abruptly the contrasting warmth of sunbaked dirt against that cool breeze fills me with an overwhelming tactile memory, fully immersing me in the past while sending the same goosebumps twenty years into the future. Relief floods my senses.

Sighing, I can smell the nearby grass, hear birds tweet and flutter about up in the branches. The sunlight flickers through the leaves of our old oak, the only tree in our secret spot, a place no one's parents ever found, sheltering countless adventures, make-shift picnics, one wobbly tree fort, and later drinking, virginity, rejection.

I shake my head, suppress the teenage memories. Nine years old. The light winks and dances across the dirt. My friends. The boy leans against the tree, legs askew, his toothy smile absorbs his face. The girl, nestled in the crook of his arm, lips closed but eyes bright, the constant half smile ready to burst into infectious laughter at any moment.

From a distance, you assume they're a couple. A few years older and certainly it's a scene of young love. Perhaps it still is, on some level, but not romantically. That field, that oak, before the complications of relationships, of expectations, hurt, disappointment. Loss. No, this was a casual intimacy we shared. Neither questioned nor appreciated, we simply experienced. It was safe. It was easy.

Always the entertainer, I dance before them. Part hula, part ballerina, all me. I sway and spin and giggle, basking in the attention of everything that matters. He throws a pile of leaves at me, she bats a few back in his face. We laugh.

There! Connected. Loved. Loving.

My breath catches. The feeling washes over me in a wave and I feel whole, if only for a moment. Inhaling fast and deep,

I strain my lungs to capacity before the feeling passes, memory and oxygen both suffusing me with life, desperately, as though I've clawed to the surface half drowned. Smiling, feeling light, I hold it in for a few seconds, relish it.

Opening my eyes, I return to reality, stare myself down in the mirror. What have you done? How did you get here?

"Whew. Suck it up buttercup." I whisper, poking my reflection on the nose.

Her smile wavers, uncertain, until a gentle frown takes hold. The feeling used to last longer, but I suppose it's fading with time, now no more than some half-remembered dream, a ghost. Ephemeral. Sighing, I shake my head at her. And no doubt romanticized.

Furrowing my brow lightly, I give her a casual appraisal while trying to finger comb long, wavy hair, my best feature. A bit messy today. And by a bit, I mean matted here and there, strays in all directions, knots galore, a veritable Jackson Pollock of hair!

I ought to brush it out before braiding, but my brush is currently MIA. Losing things in a space too small to lose anything, a specialty of mine. My shoulders loosen as I fruitlessly poke about the room, as though accepting this truth somehow brings me back into the present, brings me home. It's so me! Did unearth my Hello Kitty mug though, tucked behind my 'to read' book pile.

"Hello old friend." I say aloud, frowning at an ageless coffee stain.

Resuming the task at hand, I eyeball the mess sitting on my head. It's compounded nightly by too much hair vs. too many blankets and pillows, plus a touch of drool, one twenty-five-year-old stuffed raccoon, and an unfathomable army of cozy socks all joining the fray, each vying for territory while I wrap myself into a cocoon against the chill.

Grimacing, tugging through knots, today is the breaking point. Today I will brave town for a new brush! Having split the mess into three semi-orderly sections, I mark the finger combing a success.

The narrow, angular face in the mirror tilts her head, questioning said success, and continues to scrutinize me as I pull the emerging braid to the front. I hate her pale blue eyes, too light, flirting with grey, dull. Mom says they shine, an overcompensating compliment. Makes it worse.

I blink, wiggle my eyebrows a little, pull a few faces I imagine to be seductive. Nope. Well, maybe that look wouldn't work on humans, but an emu? That was spot-on come-hither to an emu.

The notion makes me giggle, so I turn to the window and slap my thighs, arms open in anticipation.

"Get over here you big hunk of feathers! Rawr!"

Not a single emu trotting this way! Glancing back at the mirror I see my reflection has donned a face of surprise.

Feeling loose, I put my hands on my hips and shake my head at her, "An emu? Really?"

She arches her eyebrows smugly, a subtle, 'Well, not yet.'

Wiping a few strays from my face, I poke around for a headband, mumbling, "That'd be great, a nice, stately emu would really complete the vibe around here."

Another success! My rainbow headband, sticking out of the hamper, passes a smell test.

With a sweeping gesture I bow lightly to the empty corner, "I shall call him Steven, and he shall teach me the way of the noble emu as we gallivant about in the mountains." Briefly I entertain the idea he would sport a monocle, but shake it off. Steven's too down to earth for nonsense.

Returning to the dork in the mirror, I throw my arms up, jutting a hip out ("bada-boom!"), proving once and for all my figure beats a twelve-year-old boy's! Up on tip toes, I imagine being taller, shrug, and slide into a little soft eyed, hip swinging cabaret. Yes friends, small and feisty! Too hot to handle! I stop and jazz hands at her, fingers up and gyrating about, completing the effect with a little two-step.

Nodding together, we decide that's me, we'll take her. I'm more muscle than feminine curves, I'm fit, I eat well. Society can take their make-up and shove it.

Leaning over, I palm the floor, slap my calves a few times. "You two ready? At least twenty today!" On second thought, my legs are my best feature. I was reaching, admiring the rat's nest up top. I earned these legs!

I straighten up and smile sheepishly at my kitty, who's watching from the dresser, feigning boredom despite rapt attention.

"I'm just lonely today little one. Don't look at me like that."

Unmoved, he stares, clearly judgmental with those beady, black eyes. As the feeling of my fantasy flitters across my chest, I sigh. Fine.

Raising both hands in supplication, I declare, "Avert thy gaze oh wise one! Slay me with insight no more!" Lowering my arms, I murmur, "Jerk."

Thus addressed, he stands, comes to the edge. I bend so we can touch noses. Giving him a good scratch behind the ears, he bumps his head against my cheek. Judgmental or not, he is a sweet companion. I pick him up and he nuzzles my ear as I spin in a slow circle, taking in my little home in the mountains. Four hundred square feet of peace. What more do I need?

Meeting my reflection again, we squint at each other. Panicked with the tense, sudden stop, the damn cat claws my shoulder as he leaps away and skitters into the kitchen. Attacked! I jump back, pulling finger guns at the only remaining assailant, a goofy girl in the mirror! It's a tie.

"Bang, bang," I say quietly, blowing on the tips of my pointer fingers. We smile. Examining the three angry claw marks, I figure there's a metaphor in there somewhere. No blood at least.

Flinging the braid to my back, I throw a nervous glance at the pile of camping gear laid out against the wall, uneasily muttering, "Today's long run brought to you by hearty rationalizations. Backpacking clearly uses different muscles."

After a moment I nod once, emphatically, and stride outside.

The magpies were aflutter this morning. I woke to their shrill chatter, rolled over and spotted a dozen or so through the window, urgently hopping about in the yard. I can never decide if they're angry or excited when they do that, but it's theater generally reserved for an approaching storm.

Standing on my porch, I suppose they offered a false prophecy. The breeze touches my brow lightly, cool, the season turning already, but the sky is clear. Sharp in the distance, the Rockies offer the same awe inspired calm that brought me here in the first place. An involuntary sigh escapes.

A lone magpie remains, quiet, intent on something in the scruff before my footfall grabbed his attention. He cocks his head, stares, the moment pregnant. I'm certain he nods solemnly before taking off, quickly fading into a silhouette against the mountain backdrop. Smiling, I figure I should have saluted him, or at least complimented his little tuxedo.

Sucking in the mountain air, the view, the peace, I shake off the melancholy hanging about. I tap my nose. Right. Suck it up. Bouncing on my toes a little, I offer an exaggerated wink to no one, to everyone.

Grabbing my running vest, full of snacks and water, I suddenly sprint through the yard, still fumbling to clip the vest together. No warm up today, no pace. Heedlessly the trail flies beneath, my home falling behind with its mirrors, judgmental cats, fantasy, absurdity. I am churning legs and heaving lungs, a singularity. And blissfully, there is only now. I burn.

Embracing the obliviating silence of effort, I am free.

PART I

*She held her grief behind her eyes like an ocean
and when she leaned forward into the day it spilled onto the floor
and she wiped at it quickly with her foot
and pretended no one had seen.*

"Hidden Ocean", Brian Andreas

1

Breathe.

I glance about to find myself in a rickety cabin I explored as a child. Awash with memory, I can feel the magic and mystery invoked by that bright-eyed little girl. It was all around as I tentatively tiptoed, a treasure waiting in every closet, behind every book, under a secret floorboard. Today I stand stock still, an emotional chill leaving goosebumps in its wake. Instantly familiar, yet out of place in time, the warm sunlight sparkling on the dust I've stirred. I inhale the stale, amber atmosphere. My breath catches. For a moment the walls act strangely, arching towards the depth of my morning yawn. No. Making the sound of a dying seagull, "bhrugurhubrhu!" I shake the sleep away. Is that the sound a dying seagull makes? I've never been here. Where the hell am I even? Surreal. Where's the F-ing coffee?

"Babe, did we bring coffee?"

"Mmprh."

"Coffee. Now. Function."

"Mm."

Scratching my belly, I slip back into the bedroom and fling myself onto John, snuffling him like a dog.

"Gooode mowrning John, iths's time for coooooffffeee! Did we bring coffee? Have you hidden it from me? That's it. Those are fighting words. Fisticuffs!"

"Suz. Christ! We always bring coffee. Did you even look? What time is it?"

Knowing he'll sleep another hour, I give his cheek an aggressive pat and wander kitchen-ward, throwing a wistful, "Sure would be nice to share morning coffee with someone," over my shoulder.

Course that's not really true. Morning coffee, fresh morning air, fresh everything. Best alone really. I mean, imagine John trying to 'elucidate' on the way the light flickers in the leaves, the long shadows, the breeze ruffling my shirt. Well his shirt. Who 'elucidates' anyway? Who has two thumbs and 'elucidates?' 'This guy! Ho, hor, hor!' I wish he'd make that joke, taking himself less seriously. How do I twist that around? 'Who has two thumbs and elucidates?' 'You, dipshit!' God I can see the hurt look now.

Neanderthals built this cabin, before the advent of electricity. I offer a silent prayer of thanks to the god of large white cylinders that are outdoor propane tanks, and put on water for a pour over.

Waking, I am actually a bit confused on how we got here. A gap in time. Maybe there'll be a wrinkle and I'll crawl through the wardrobe, become a Hufflepuff or something.

I glance at John's backpack, neatly leaned against the bookshelf, a bastion of orderly packing. A downright manual. Role your undies like so, your socks like such, the shirts in a V shape, wah-lah, 0.002 extra cubic inches! The coffee, of course, pre ground in the blue Tupperware, second front pocket on the right. Hm, the vibrator on the left, a man of priorities. Tempting way to wake up, but I'll stick with the coffee on this fine morning. Can still smell last night's romp on me. If I knew where I'd packed extra panties (did I?), be a good idea. Actually, John probably has a pair stashed somewhere. That, my friends, makes me smile.

Settling onto the kitchen floor, I savor the rough wood against my legs. A long stretch, a sigh. Content, I listen for the water to boil, I take in a breeze through open windows, I drift. Magic.

❦

"Susan?" lilting, my mother.

"Susan, darling? Are you ok?" Tap, tap. Knock. Tentative.

"Ah, just finishing up!" turning on the water.

No. No I am not ok. Who am I? Both hands on the sink. Stable. Solid. I squeeze the porcelain a bit, run my thumb over the cool metal border, build the courage to look up. There you are. Ok. Not so bad. I look totally the same.

Letting out an aggressive sigh I fluff my bangs, making me laugh. Takes me back to stealing Alice's hairdryer, lips and cheeks fluttering like a crazed puffer fish, hair straight up and dancing. People have sex all the time. No big deal. In fact, I've just gotten an adult merit badge.

❦

I snap to, angry water splashing the blue propane flames. Popping up I fumble into John's backpack for the coffee, grabbing my Hello Kitty mug and pour over filter in the process. So much for listening for the water to boil. Why didn't I measure the coffee before daydream time?

Odd space on that one. It's not like my virginity was traumatic. Ethan was sweet, stumbling along, actually worried about me. Could have dated first I guess, or been sober, but no, I've got no complaints. You hear all these horror stories, and I'm just like, yeah, I lost mine to a childhood friend who loved me from the time we were seven. Broke his heart of course, but who's counting? You can't stay with the first. That's like, eh, like having one kind of taco your whole life. There are all kinds of epic tacos out there! Sure, I'd have enjoyed that one for a while if I hadn't been so terrified, but c'mon, we were kids. Besides, a few bland tacos are essential to appreciating a good one, plus the bad ones are so safe. Throw away a violent, insecure taco, everyone wins! Find the best taco ever, and it's nothing but work, work, work, making sure to keep the taco around. I just can't spend my life worrying about taco accessibility.

A totally decent, albeit not that challenging, taco? That's a winner. Wish mine would drag his sweet ass out of bed right about now. I'll stir him up wafting some coffee in his face. He'll have to get his own damn cup, but that'll get him moving. Maybe.

2

Heavy footsteps mark the belated arrival of a yawning and bleary eyed John, mumbling, "Hm. Morning Suz. Been up long?"

"Ah! The beast arises!" Stumbling around the deck, I grunt and scratch. "Smell woman! A great pheromonal call hath drug me from slumber!"

My arms raised, getting excited. "From whence doth this intoxication smolder? A peach! A soft sweetly tangy flower! Ah! Forsooth! The exquisite goddess Susan Marie hath called me hither. My soul awakens; I am forsaken. I am yours!"

"Cute," running a hand down my back, smiling, "Actually I believe the smell of coffee called me hither. Lovely out eh?"

John is strikingly attractive. Tall, sharp featured, his dark, always messy hair offset by crystal blue eyes. His usual scratchy shadow of what could be a thick beard, filled in more than normal today. Seeing him in his standard hoodie and shorts, the outline of his chest still visible through the layers, I always feel a twinge of girlish excitement. Yes, casually muscled legs, you just want to chew on them a little! The fastidiousness of his entire personality extends well into the physical regiment of running, swimming and weights. I'm not certain I really fit him, being anything but fastidious, but I reap the benefits, and we love running together. Well, to be fair I think I entertain him. Loose in a way he can't permit himself to be, but enjoys being around.

Placing my hand on his chest, I lean in, close my eyes. Comfort as he tousles my hair distractedly, looking out at the trees. I stand on my tip toes and kiss him lightly.

"I made you a cup, should still be hot."

Squeezing me for a moment, he rubs my back again and plants a kiss in my hair, "That's nothing short of spectacular. Thanks gorgeous. Sorry I was grumpy earlier." He heads back inside, follows his nose.

"You're always grumpy in the morning," I call after him, "That's the fun of it! Come back and sit with me. There's a double porch swing."

Rocking gently, I know he'll have to get in a workout soon, but he's mine for now. Curled into the Suz-nook of his right arm, legs flung across his lap, I note the swing's remarkably well maintained for a deserted cabin, with clean, comfy cushions and a shiny new chain.

"John," I mumble softly, "Do you remember Ethan?"

"Of course. it's my solemn duty as Alpha Male to have a passing knowledge of all your sexual escapades, especially concerning the guy you grew up with who claimed your virginity."

"Heh, no I mean really remember him, not know of him. Wasn't he in your Economics class or something?"

"Ah, English actually, Junior year I think. No, I never knew him. I sought him out at a party once, after I met you, doing a little Susan reconnaissance, and putting a face to your history. It wasn't until then that I even realized we were in a class together." Smiling down at me he adds, "Seemed like a pretty cool guy while we shot the shit, but somehow asking about you dampened his enthusiasm."

This amuses me. The idea of John and Ethan drinking together at a party, silently appraising each other while discussing *The Old Man and the Sea* or something. In my mind, two gorillas scratching and bumping chests, John the Silverback, Ethan small but brave, not backing down, proud. Suddenly I picture Ethan's courage winning John over, the silverback affectionately cuffing him, dancing excitedly and offering a handful of the best berries. If only.

"Why? Got him on the mind? You really should call him and reconnect. Rachel too. It's like you've thrown away the idyllic childhood everyone else wishes they had."

The mention of Rachel expands the lump in my throat, "My childhood was hardly idyllic." I ruffle John's hair, still picturing him as a Silverback. "Something about this cabin reminds me of him. Can't place it though."

Grabbing my hand, he casually nibbles at my fingers, like he's reading my mind and playacting the gorilla. "Come on Suz, your father aside, everything I hear about your childhood would make Disney proud. Few people have connections that deep at such a young age."

Unamused, my face flat, I stare out at the trees. After a moment I remind him, "John, I don't have a father," maybe a little more aggressively than intended. Quietly I add, "His choice, not mine."

He sits motionless, still holding my fingers to his lips. John knows better than to push the subject and patiently waits for me to settle.

Giving him a pass for bringing it up, I steer us back, "Most Disney childhoods are pretty tragic actually, setting up the redemption. Anyway, depth was the problem, doomed us to implode. Some connections are not meant to last."

"I dunno Suz," dropping my hand, "You're all adults now. I think you'd be surprised."

I'm silent a minute, increasingly uncomfortable with where this is heading. I take a deep breath, deciding to steer us in a direction I'm certain will annoy him. I don't relish the idea, but I need to bring it up. Better than talking about Rachel or Ethan at least.

"John," I pause, staring off into the trees, "How did we get here?"

"Us specifically? The way your hips blinded my sensibilities, inspiring one awkwardly fortuitous sticky note *despite* having to carry your sloppy drunk ass up the stairs, coffee, hikes, runs, and finally you sealing the deal with the gradual seepage of Suz inner dialog? Or is this breezy peace inspiring a deeper question? The human condition? The great metaphorical debate!" Raising one hand to the sky, emphatically, "How?"

The relationship synopsis makes me smile, though he never lets me forget how hammered I was the night we met. "Ah, well, both interesting. But, mm, no." Sitting up a bit, stealing a cushion for my back, I lean against the armrest to look his way more directly. "I mean literally. Like how did we get to this cabin?"

This grabs his attention, eyeing me quizzically, wearily. "Is this one of those Suz questions I'm too square to understand? I don't feel like playing that game today. Not here."

"No, no. Sorry. I just don't really remember exactly. I feel a little confused." Playing with his fingertips, his hand resting on my left thigh.

A sigh, taking his hand away, placing it on the back of the swing. "Have you eaten today? Do you think your blood sugar is ok?" John, ever the healthcare layman, with just enough googling to be dangerous.

"My blood sugar is fine. I don't think it works that way babe, I'm not diabetic. Humor me."

I can sense his slight exasperation, like I'm tainting the peaceful cabin experience asking him to do something he doesn't understand. I should drop it, but the time gap gnaws along the edges of reality. Something is not quite right. A favorite song flittering in the sub-conscious recesses I can't quite access. My long dead grandmother's face not quite remembered. It's there, but lost in time. I can't fully put it together. But yesterday. Yesterday shouldn't feel so detached! I wait, staring past him quietly. I'll win this one, our time together definitely includes his regularly humoring me.

Finally, tired of waiting for him to decide he can't figure me out, I prompt, "We were backpacking?"

Big sigh this time. "Yes, we're backpacking. Though I'd say this cabin is definitely cheating."

A robin lights on the deck's railing. Hopping along, taking us in side eyed. No food here friend. John stops the swing gently with his toes, sitting quietly we share the moment. The robin, feeling unthreatened, preens jerkily, hops a few more inches, suddenly takes off at the sound of a chipmunk in the leafy detritus below.

Knowing I'm still waiting he gives up. "Of course Suz can't stick to a planned route, but as per usual we really lucked out with this distraction." Now he's offering half a smile my way. He's always bemused when my haphazard approach finds more reward than his carefully outlined plans. The smile creeps across his face as we process this same thought. He laughs, shakes his head at the chipmunk.

"Hey little guy, does your chipmunk lady ignore all logical odds, yet somehow make your life better in the process?" Seeming to understand he's being addressed, the chipmunk leans back on his haunches, blinking our way, paused mid thought, a nut in paw.

Chuckling at me now, amused with himself. "I'd already passed the trail. If I didn't know better, I'd say it wasn't even there. I mean, I'm always alert to the risk of missing a turn! But you saw it, buried under overgrowth, vines and branches."

I smile at him, the description sounding vaguely familiar. I take his hand and place it back on my thigh where it belongs. He smiles too, an apology behind the crinkle in his eyes. I love it when he relaxes into not quite understanding me.

"And that sign! Creepy, intriguing and absolutely irresistible all at once. You brushed the kudzu aside and immediately we exchanged a glance, eyebrows up in unison. I mean, who names a trail, or location, or whatever that sign was supposed to demark, after a literary term? In the middle of freaking nowhere, the trail overgrown, obscured. All so fitting somehow! Ha! And what the fuck did they mean by it? Freedom from society? Responsibility? I mean, we already had those things just being out in the backcountry, backpacking, without some fancy cabin. Rescued from ourselves perhaps? Each other? Heh."

Shaking his head again, "It almost feels like a different layer entirely. Sinister maybe."

Furrowing his brow, he actually shudders. I can tell he finds something not quite right about all this too, but he smiles with the adventure. I've never seen John shudder. He's excited now though, leaning forward in the swing, making me sigh. Drawing this version of John to the surface and I fall for him all over again.

"By then I couldn't have passed it up either, and was just pumped you spotted it! And here we are, a short hike later, nearly a bushwhack really, the trail so disused. An immaculate cabin, water running, propane available, sheets on the bed. Bit dusty maybe, but fairly clean. See the sign above the door?"

I look up. In elaborate script the door tells us:

You Are Here
All Who Seek
All Who Wander
-- And Wonder --
You Are Welcome

I gape at the sign. That I know! I'm certain. I've seen that quote before. In that very script! But Jesus Jumping Christ, where? This place is driving me crazy.

I turn back to John, afraid to taint his enthusiasm with my distraction. He can tell I don't remember the trail sign, but now he's savoring the suspense, enjoying my curiosity and complete engagement in his retelling.

I thump him on the chest, "Well? What did the trail say?!"

He laughs, still bemused, gesturing to the cabin, the trees, breathes deep for a moment, winks at the still watching chipmunk.

"Deus Ex Machina."

The chipmunk cocks his head, oddly attentive. The air grows still, shadows deepening with a passing cloud. The robin peers at us intently. A wave shudders the trees, almost seaweed swaying underwater, and sound closes off around me, like the cabin of an airplane pressurizing. The powerful mirage sends a small chill head to toe, dizzying. I close my eyes to stop the dancing trees, but this only enhances the sensation of forced silence, of isolation. There it is again, the feeling of something lost, but present. Just out of reach. Something my subconscious knows, keeping trapped below sea level. I shake it off, looking up at John, and sound returns with the creak of the swing. His eyes are closed, fully content, basking in the feeling all around us. The cabin, the trees, sunlight, the magic and mystery of our hidden discovery.

The chipmunk chews his nut, the robin busies himself in the dirt, a seed in reach. Of course they were never watching. I chastise myself for anthropomorphizing the locals, a side effect of the disquieting sensations washing over me, imbued by unexplained confusion in this remarkable, beautiful, enchanting spot. My imagination tends to run full speed ahead, unbridled.

Something about this place. Nostalgic.

3

Back on the porch swing, I must have fallen asleep after lunch. Isn't that what the warm breeze, porch swing combo is for? My hair tickles across my nose and I smile at John brushing it aside, pleased that he must have been watching and seen my nose crinkle.

My eyes are still closed when the swing jerks as he stands cradling me in his arms, impressive in one fluid motion without the slightest grunt. Nuzzling into his neck I know what this means, and the warmth washes straight down between my legs.

Though I don't exactly remember, my panties testify we had sex last night, so this is an unexpected bonus! It's been some time since we followed an evening romp with an afternoon encore. Must be this place, this adventure. Sex, love, that's all part of seeking, wandering and wondering right? Well, or just being away from stress, work, deadlines.

I'm still overthinking it, analyzing how I can reproduce this desire later, once he's laid me in bed and pulled off my shirt. He can tell I'm not present. Pausing, he waits for me to open my eyes. Peering down into them, his crystal blues shine excitedly. No, lovingly. Both. Mine actually water. God, I love this man. He knows! For a moment this is truly terrifying, but it passes.

We're lost in it together.

༺༻

Sweaty, satiated, I listen to his steady breathing, asleep. Smiling, I sigh and give myself a mental high five, stealthily slipping out of bed.

Hm, I could definitely use a shower, "Yowzah! This girl's got bite!" I proclaim to no one in particular, lifting my arms in defiance, taking a deep whiff while gyrating my hips about in a little jig.

"Heh, whew." Enough of that. Shaking my head, I marvel all the more that John's bedded me twice in this state. I loved his smell just now, but didn't think about my own. Coloring a little at the notion, I file that away for further research. Pheromones for the win! Exquisite goddess indeed. Shower time.

My gently ripe self makes me wonder how many days we've been backpacking. The hole in my memory's still a bit disconcerting, but at this point I'm too content to do anything but accept it. Chuckling I wonder if I should loot my pack, tabulating the dirty clothes with a smell test to estimate their use. I've pushed my luck enough asking John. He'd be convinced I'm sporting a brain tumor if I admitted the entire trip is blank before today. Besides, I don't dare hint I've forgotten having sex with him last night. He'd be crushed his magic penis couldn't penetrate the fog. Men.

Eyes closed, fingers crossed, I gently turn the 'H' faucet in the bathroom sink and hold my breath. After only moments of suspense, I am eternally grateful to register the presence of hot water!

Yes, it turns out electricity is for suckers. What do I need, my phone charged and buzzing away? Shuddering at the idea of external world intrusions, this time I blow a kiss in the general direction of the Propane God.

Catching my smiling reflection in the mirror, I jiggle my breasts at her out of general principle, literally a small feat given the tennis ball halves I smuggle around. She squints at my chest a moment, something there?, then concedes the point. Perky!

Stacks of blue and pink towels adorn a rather ornate bookshelf shoved tightly between the toilet and sink. Always the rebel, I place a blue one on the rack. A fluffy bathroom rug feels luxurious under my bare feet, but I feel a twinge of guilt at the contrast of my dirty, sweat streaked feet against the rug's perfect white.

I step off the rug on tip toes to balance in the narrow space next to the shower, leaning a hand on the towel rack. Oddly, using my hand for support makes my forearm ache sharply, and I examine it for bruising. As per usual I'm sure I banged it on something.

Noticing how bright the room is I look up at a large skylight overseeing my awkward stance. Taking it in, really this is a well-appointed and inviting guest bathroom. The skylight is streaked with dirt though.

"Not sufficiently motivated to climb onto the roof and clean the skylights, eh Alfred?" (as I've decided the cabin's owner is surely named Alfred). "Well I'll simply have to complain to management. Truly. Clean sheets and towels are one thing, but a girl's got to have standards, even in a strange cabin hidden in the woods."

After the usual fumbling over a new shower's functionality, I'm in and it. Is. Glorious! Both hands on the wall, I watch the thin layer of grime washing down the drain. At least four days' worth I think, longer if we got in a lake or river. Scraping my thumb across an armpit, a gross amount of stubble seems to confirm ballpark four days as reasonable. Feeling Sherlock Holmesee, I tell myself four days of amnesia is nothing to worry about.

Happens all the time, right? I was probably hiking along with my silly sunhat on, watching the ground for trip hazards and blissfully unaware John had ducked a low hanging branch. One of those at the perfect height, thick as my waist, waiting in anxious anticipation. Smack! I'd done it a few times. Threw the sunhat into a creek once, before guiltily retrieving it, stashing it, and finally putting it back on the next sunlit section. Skin cancer is no joke. Fleetingly I wonder if Alfred has guest razors stashed somewhere.

With a start I see John's stuck his head through the curtain and followed my eyes to the drain.

"You are a dirty girl! My favorite kind!" A mischievous smile. "Hot water too huh? Wow."

He looks me up and down, appraising my naked body in the way men do. I should feel objectified, but I can't help but enjoy his obvious approval. Reaching in he tugs my pubic hair gently, leaning in to kiss my breasts. Jerking the shower head onto him I laugh and dance away, spraying the bathroom floor briefly before he can snap the curtain shut.

"Back beast! This gentle maiden is not yours to plunder!" Flinging water over the shower rod I yell, "The power of Christ compels you! The power of Christ compels you!"

Jovial, he barks a laugh, "Touché! Uncle! You're soaking the rug out here."

Reappearing at the back of the shower, he brushes my lips lightly with his thumb, holding my cheek a moment. "The trail can wait, let's stay here another night or two. I'll head out for a run instead. Ok?"

I nod silently, grateful. I'm glad he knew I wasn't up for a run. I probably could have motivated to power hike with him if his itinerary required it, but this luxury has consumed my desire.

"Suz?" Waiting to draw my attention, "I love you." A smile. A wink. And he's gone.

My eyes are busy watering again. Feeling like a sap I scrub my face roughly. Slowing, I chastise myself for the aggression and pause, allowing at least a brief savoring of his affection, a sentiment I don't hear too often. This overwhelms me though, and sinking down I sit heavily on the shower floor.

Cradling my knees, the hot spray on the back of my neck, I let out a long sigh and whisper, "I love you too."

Staring blankly, tears quietly tracking their way to my legs, I know reticence with affection is merely my own, and reflects his patience with me. I've never actually said those words to him. I've said it to a few others before, but falling for John makes it clear I never meant it.

I try to practice again, gathering courage to mumble simple words his way. Nothing comes out. The water beats down relentlessly.

4

Totally refreshed. A shower after a few days, ahem four days right?, is truly a lovely feeling. I've consented to one of Alfred's pink towels to wrap my long hair, laying the blue one on the floor of the living area, sitting cross legged, naked and happy. I've got two hours easy before John gets back. Loves to trail run. I try to meditate for a minute, but too many thoughts intrude. I look around the room and take it in.

Kitchen, living room, bedroom, bathroom, all small. Wood burning fireplace in here, complete with a stack of firewood. Probably do need power for propane heat I guess.

Always a voracious reader, I get up to check out the bookshelf, flinging the pink towel onto the blue. Classics mostly, all old. *Of Mice and Men, Lord of The Flies*, Oliver Fucking Twist. Nothing I read really.

I'm excited to find a framed photograph tucked away, shelved sideways like a book. Feeling like a sleuth I fumble it out, brushing the dust away. I lean on the shelf for stability, momentarily staring directly into my past. Rachel!

It's not her though, of course, she's just on the mind since John brought her up. Looking again, she could be some cousin of Rachel's they favor each other so. Same shoulder length blond hair blowing in the wind, same round girlish cheeks, same smile curving into high cheekbones, framing her dark brown eyes, this girl throwing a full-bodied laugh at the cameraman. I smile remembering Rachel's infectious laugh, and then chuckle out loud, the memory having the same effect. Course she generally wore a half smile, analogous to the way she saw the world.

I close my eyes, conjuring my old best friend in full. Thin but much curvier than I am, with actual breasts boys were always trying to paw, ironically. Constellations of freckles across her cheeks and nose, which were lovely, but she always covered with make-up from about fourteen on. Though she'd deny it, we all knew she was the attractive one in our little threesome. Looking down at the picture, I think she's Alfred's wife maybe, a lover at least, with real intimacy in her stance and eyes.

All told, the picture provides a slight chill up my spine, once again feeling my past creeping close about me in this place. Rachel and I had a massive falling out. A little teenage experimentation and oops, nothing's ever the same. Our friendship might have survived, but it meant so much more to her. I couldn't face that! So yeah, I lashed out, belittled it. Ethan and I didn't really talk anymore, but he sought me out to confront me, defend her. Looking back, I bet he'd known how she felt for years. Certain he would pass on the message, I flatly told him I tried on the lesbian hat, it didn't fit, and I couldn't believe how disgusting it was. 'I can't even look at her, makes me want to fucking puke.' Christ. I am horrible.

Looking closer, Rachel's doppelganger is standing on the edge of a rather dramatic cliff. Not much for heights myself, it makes me uncomfortable, but she looks right at home.

Rachel was like that. Brave. Must have taken guts to kiss me, seventeen years old, breaking that solemn barrier, forever altering our friendship. For a long time I resented her, blaming her for the loss of our connection. I see now she felt she had to try. Knowing the gamble, rolling the dice anyway. Guilt washes over me. I should have been kinder about it somehow.

What, twelve years ago now? Lost. Stamping my foot I say aloud, "I will call you when I get home." A resolution I've made before, but John's right, and for the first time I feel like I really mean it!

Our parents are still friends. Last I heard she was doing a post-doc somewhere, having finished her doctorate. Mathematics, something about fractals, whatever that is. Mom always gives me the updates on Rachel and Ethan, unabashedly pushing the hope her youngest will reconnect with childhood friends. I know she envisions a backyard barbeque with all of us and our families, she the matriarch, sitting with her friends of twenty plus years, surrounded by children and grandchildren. A scene she first dreamed up when the three of us became inseparable.

That night with Rachel was one of the most intense of my young life, for a multitude of reasons. I've never thought about it much, dismissing it with a shudder any time the thought touched my consciousness, blocking uncomfortable, overwhelmed, broken hearted, locking the night away deep inside, where it's safe. Where I'm safe.

Today feels different. Today I'm ready to be brave and unlock the door, channeling Rachel's bravery for inspiration. I know I need to deal with it if I'm actually going to reconnect. Ok. Taking another glance at the doppelganger, I put on Rachel's half smile and try to relax my bunched-up shoulders. Closing my eyes, I drift into our last night as friends.

❧❧

The party has broken up. We're both buzzed, lounging on a couch, happy to be left alone in each other's company.

"Seriously, he tried to kiss me." Her eyes alight, laughing.

"Steve? Dumb as a brick, strutting around in his basketball jersey, sleeping through class in a puddle of drool, Steve?" I'm incredulous. "What is he, like 6'8"? Bet he's hung at least."

Rachel play slaps me on the shoulder, "It was really sweet actually, if it weren't for the dumb as a brick part."

I raise my eyebrows at her. Steve and sweet are incongruous.

"Honestly. We were just talking, humoring him about some basketball dunk or something, and I guess he got tired of leaning over. He picked me up around the waist and gently set me up on the bar. Like I weighed nothing at all! I was so startled I didn't know what to say. He was befuddled too, at his audacity in touching me that way, and for a moment I thought he was drunk enough to just wander off, embarrassed. But instead he smiled shyly, and gets in front of me like this."

At this point Rachel gets on her knees on the floor in front of me, softly easing my legs apart with her hips and sliding between them.

Laying her hand on my cheek, she says, "he really amped up his courage here, looking me right in the eyes and giving me this little speech, obviously rehearsed. 'You are the most beautiful girl I have ever seen, and you are remarkably intelligent, endearingly funny, invariably kind. I've been psyching myself up all night to do this.'"

I catch my breath a little, not sure how to take being in this intimate space with her, drunkenly play acting or not. I know she feels it too.

"I think he was giving me a moment to respond to this declaration, but I didn't know what the fuck to say! So he slips his other hand to the small of my back, like this, and pulls me into him, my butt sliding easily across the countertop. Slow, giving me plenty of time to stop the obvious progression, but with a little plea in his eyes."

On a couch instead of a counter, I have to scooch forward to mimic the closeness, with her hand on my back, guiding me along. She's whispering to me now. My heart rabbit like, trying to leap out of my chest, and I'm just sufficiently conscious of the situation to wonder if the story is true at all, or her own carefully rehearsed scene playing out with me. Dimly the absurdity of Steve acting this way flickers across my mind, the impossibility of using phrases like 'invariably kind.'

"And he leans in, his cheek against mine, like this."

I have no thought of stopping it.

"He pulls me tighter," she breathes, "pressing his body between my legs, inhaling lightly against my cheek as he turns," a little gulp of breath from her, "as he turns to meet my lips."

And we're kissing. Holy shit I'm kissing my best friend Rachel! My head's spinning from the alcohol, from pent up emotions I can't quite grasp, from a rush of... of something remarkable against her flat belly pressed between my legs!

She crawls off the floor onto the couch with me, never letting go of the back of my neck, fingers in my hair, our lips gently locked, sitting between my spread legs and wrapping hers around me. Truly making out now, I'm thinking how soft she is, how nice it is to share this intensity without having a tongue shoved down my throat, immediately groped.

We kiss for a long time, though time has stopped. Eventually, she's stroking my breasts, teasing blissfully hard nipples lightly through my bra. Suddenly I feel her shudder and gasp, a moan escaping, and I realize she's been rolling her hips against me, gently massaging herself on my leather belt buckle.

Flushed, panting even, locking her eyes on mine, she scooches back and unbuttons my shorts. I am sopping wet, soaking through panties, shorts, a spot on the couch. She slips a finger inside me, pressing her palm to my clit, and I gasp. I know I can come if I let it happen, but abruptly the old terror rushes in, a freight train screeching No! No! NO! through my brain. I grab her wrist violently!

For an odd moment I think of Ethan, looking me in the eyes, asking me if it's ok as he slips inside. In an even more disconnected moment, surrounded by the smell and closeness of my oldest friend Rachel, my addled brain feels we're kids again, wrestling and I'm pretending to give her an Indian rug burn.

She stops of course, gently pulling her hand out of my pants, her palm glistening, finger covered. I watch with a twinge of panic as she wraps her lips around the length of her finger, closing her eyes, savoring, yet stealing one more step of intimacy from me.

Crawling off, kissing my neck on the way, she leans on the couch and watches me curiously, no doubt wondering how her big play will pan out. I have to resist flinching from the final kiss, and stand up stiffly.

Looking back, our eyes lock momentarily as friends for the last time, her easy smile bringing mine out for company. I leave her on the couch, shiver in the bathroom for a bit, eventually call a cab. She's asleep as I'm leaving, a contented smile playing across her lips.

I fumble at the door, still drunk. This moment's distraction opens another door, sealing our broken friendship. Awoken behind me, she sends a love letter, stamped, earnestly mailed, strawberry perfumed with the taste of her lips, complete with understanding, compassion and a plea, backed by ten years growing up together. All at once I'm overwhelmed with every laugh, every smile, the years culminating into something more than connection, her confusing desires as we move into puberty, the way she looks at me as we whisper about boys, eventually love, LOVE, feelings blossoming unchecked throughout our inseparable and ideal friendship. She rolls it all into a neat little package as she breathes my name.

"Suzy."

I pause at the door, stunned, doorknob in hand. A moment of decision I still feel frozen in time. I walk out. I do not look back.

∽᷂᷊᷒᷉᷅

Returning to the present, still leaning on the shelf with picture in hand, I'm surprised to find I've dripped onto my left leg. Flushing, I look around guiltily at no one, snatching the blue towel off the floor.

5

Definitely had to get dressed, the little exploration with Rachel leaving me feeling vulnerable. Good though, I feel good. Suddenly I'm not certain why I avoided thinking about it for so many years. Heaven forbid my best friend fell in love with me. Well, both of my best friends. Tough problem to have, being so goddamn desirable!

Fighting suitors off left and right, I make a little kick at the couch, "Back, you!" A karate chop to the armrest for good measure, point made.

Holding the almost-Rachel picture in front of me, "Rachel, I'm sorry." I take a deep breath. "I'm sorry I couldn't love you the way you loved me. I miss you."

Too direct? I'm not sure, but it feels like a good start. I put the picture on the top shelf, facing out prominently. From a few feet away, it does look like Rachel, and all at once the cabin feels more like home.

Briefly I wonder where I might find an Ethan doppelganger, as the shelf looks incomplete without it. I feel better than I have in years. This cabin is magical after all!

"Alfred? Your magic cabin is healing my past. I'm ready to deal with Ethan now. Hellooo?"

I jump into the doorway of the bedroom, half expecting to see a picture frame hidden under the bed.

No dice. With a sigh I admit I'm simply enjoying being out of cell service, giving me the space to believe I actually will make some calls. I try to imagine sitting in the living room at home, cell phone in hand, first calling mom to get their long-deleted numbers, who then has to call their parents. Then I'm really committed. She calls me back, diligently I write down the numbers, she's excited. 'Thanks mom!' 'Good luck honey! Let me know how it goes!' Taking a deep breath, actually dialing Rachel or Ethan. Heart in throat. Might vomit. Maybe I should get drunk first? Even worse. Cowardly.

One thing at a time my friend, you apologized to a fake picture. Excellent! Baby steps!

I am in fact feeling motivated for a real baby step, opening up to John about it. At least some surface scratching, maybe more. He has a way of making me comfortable, unthreatened. He's understanding, he's an excellent sounding board, he won't try to make me commit to any actual action.

Ok. I've talked myself into it. Where is he anyway?

I wander into the kitchen, looking for a clock. Fishing John's altimeter out of his pack, which also shows the time, I see 1845, uh 6:45. I stare at it for a moment, recalculating the military time. 6:45. So much later than I thought! He left at maybe 3? 2:30? I should have looked. He should have given me some kind of plan!

Abruptly I'm feeling panicky. This is stupid on both our parts, out here in the middle of nowhere. Course he doesn't know I don't remember the trail at all. I'm not even sure what state we're in. Fuck.

A four-hour trail run. Not that long really, by his standards, but even as I try to convince myself I know he would never leave me here that long, or be out this close to evening on unfamiliar trails. No. Something has happened.

Outside now, my mind rolling, trying to form a plan of action. I smack the railing hard enough to hurt. Twice. A chipmunk scurries into the trees and vanishes, drawing attention to the nearly black veil two feet into the tree cover. It's fucking dusk.

"Of course it's fucking late!" I'm yelling at no one, "How could I not notice the change in lighting in a cabin without electricity!? I'm busy reminiscing about high school, joking about a magic cabin and a magic Alfred, and John's out there with a fucking broken ankle or something!" Pacing the deck, hands clasped tightly behind my neck.

It's cool out, going to be cold. Hurriedly I change into tights and wool socks, while trying to down some calories for dinner, stuffing my mouth with trail mix, my pockets with dried fruit and granola bars. My cell phone battery is dead, but I pocket it anyway. I grab my puffy jacket, headlamp, Garmin GPS watch from my running gear. On second thought I dump most of my backpack onto the floor so I can take it with a full water bladder. I'm sure John went out only with his handheld water bottle, he'll be dehydrated as hell. I empty the food I just stuffed into my pockets into the main compartment of my pack. Toss in my rain jacket, his puffy, fuck, toss in my sleeping bag. What else? What else? Shouldering the mostly empty pack, I head out.

I hear the robin chirping behind me. Turning to look, I watch it flutter onto the sign.

You Are Here
All Who Seek
All Who Wander
-- And Wonder --
You Are Welcome

"Right. Well I'll be back."

6

On the main trail I feel a modicum of relief. It is near impossible to spot the trail to the cabin, John probably knows he's passed by and is somewhere close combing the trees for it. I yell his name while looking for something to clearly identify the cabin trail.

Thoroughly marked with two big branches and a pile of sticks, a downright trip hazard, I look in both directions. I'm certain he headed off on new trail, but frustratingly I don't remember which direction we originally came from.

I close my eyes. Based on his story of finding the cabin trail, it sounds like we were facing the 'Deus Ex Machina' sign. Nodding my head once, I set my Garmin to track miles and stride on past the sign.

∽◌∾

Nothing. I walk. I yell. I am hoarse. It is fully dark and a black, moonless night, my headlamp illuminating a narrow band along the trail. I jump at rustling sounds in the woods, unfamiliar with being this alone, not knowing where I am. I stop and take a breath.

I am scared.

Hours pass. My watch shows I've walked six miles and I'm forced to debate if I should turn back for the cabin. Maybe I'm going the wrong direction, and by now he's there worrying about me. All I can think is that he's hurt. Nothing could have kept him out past dark, knowing I was waiting. Nothing. It feels like I'm going the right way, and backtracking could mean leaving him out overnight! Sighing, I press on.

My headlamp flickers. Still no moon. Should have grabbed John's headlamp, he always puts in fresh batteries. I smack it once, twice. It dies.

The tree cover is thick. Darkness. Complete and total. I wave my hand in my face, there but faint, ill defined. I jazz hands at the ghosts all around. No way I'm going anywhere in this.

"Fuck you." I whisper, without conviction. This I realize, is a moment I'll look back on as the most terrified I've ever been. A good story perhaps. Surely a happy ending. 'I sat down right in the middle of the trail, and five minutes later John tripped over me!'

Ok, breathe. I count ten full, slow breaths, meditative. There's really nothing to be scared of. Knowing animals take the path of least resistance too, I step just off the trail, pulling my sleeping bag out of my pack. I sit down and wrap it around my shoulders, still too ill at ease to actually get in it and restrict leg movement.

I sit for a while, feeling detached in the darkness, debating what I should have done differently. Noticing the time earlier, preparing for my rescue mission longer, staying closer to the cabin, both headlamps! I sigh. I don't know what I'm doing.

An owl's hoot startles me out of my reverie, sounding quite close in the darkness. I glance about at nothing, tuning in to subtle and unidentifiable rustles all around. It's going to be a long night.

Finally, I convince myself sleeping here on the side of the trail is best, and no different than cowboy camping without a tent. I lay back, crawl in my bag. I feel guilty John is out there somewhere, shivering. Eventually, I fall into a fitful, shallow sleep.

స్త్ర

Dawn. Grateful I can see again, I take in my surroundings. I slept directly on tree rot and fungus, and with disgust I wipe a white ooze from my cheek. I can see the paper now 'brave citizen seeks boyfriend lost in woods, catches flesh eating fungus. Dies in his arms two days later.' Holding me close in the hospital, 'Suz, I was in the bedroom the whole time, why didn't you look?' I touch his cheek gently, 'John, that goddamn chipmunk led me astray.' I breathe my last. Final words wasted on a chipmunk. Somehow this all feels fitting.

Shaking away the fantasy I jump up, packing my sleeping bag. Away from the tree rot, the air is fresh and clean, and I feel hopeful. I'm sure John weathered the night better than I did, broken bones or not. Ever the optimist, he's probably smiling, anticipating the challenge of crawling back to the cabin, and the subsequent story of triumph he'll earn to tell his friends. The competitor in me doesn't want to be a footnote in this story. 'And then Suz showed up two hours later. Where you been hon?'

Munching some dried mango, I figure at the earliest John left at two and would have run max an hour and a half in one direction, knowing he shouldn't push the daylight. Easy trail. We'll say ten minutes per mile. Ok, so nine miles, maybe more. I've been eight point two per the watch. I should be right on top of his turn around point. Being this far out already, I decide to walk a bit further. I'm confident he would have stayed on the main trail to avoid getting lost. Haven't seen any side trails anyway.

I keep wanting to turn around, then convincing myself he's right around the corner. Finally I hit ten miles. No way he set out for more than twenty. I begin to head back at a trot. The pack is too loose not to chafe but I don't care. Ten trail miles. Two hours and change at an easy jog/walk. Let's do it.

Hot. The sun easing towards mid-afternoon. My watch reads twenty-two miles. I'm exhausted and should have reached the cabin, but I kept going in disbelief, giving my watch a wide margin for error. No way I missed all those branches marking the cabin trail! Would some animal move them? Did Alfred come back, huffing and offended to find his secret hideaway marked, angrily tossing them into the woods?

Stopping, I tear up. Still not a single side trail! It's as if I'm in a loop, following the same mile over and over, flat, easy, tree lined.

"Fuck you Alfred! Do I look like I'm done with your magic cabin?" My yell startling a nearby robin into flight.

Throwing my pack against a boulder, I sit heavily. I'm piling mistakes on top of each other! I feel lost, a worst-case scenario.

I do a quick inventory. A granola bar, some more dried mango, a few ounces of water. Pulling the water bladder out of the pack, eyeing it warily, 4 ounces, maybe 6. Do I head back looking for the cabin? It's good to stay put when lost, but no one is looking for me. I'm the one looking for John for Christ's sakes!

Resting my head in my hands, I do not know what to do. "Fuck! Fuckity, fuck, fuck fuck!"

Flustered, I sit quietly, giving myself ten minutes to rest, calm down, refocus. I let my mind go blank and wait for inspiration. Calming, I acknowledge the lovely weather, peaceful trail. Any other situation this would feel amazing. Breathe.

I do not need to find the cabin. I need to find John. I'm sure I'll cross a stream or something, and without any way to treat the water I can brave a little giardia. Food is no big deal.

Standing, I brush off some dirt, scratch my scalp, bounce from foot to foot like I'm getting ready for a race. I'm tired, but I've done ultra-marathons. This is nothing. Easy trail. Everything's under control. I got this!

Cupping my hands around my mouth, I make a crowd going wild noise like John would, "Hhhaaahhh! Hahhhhh!" and channel his exuberant announcer voice, "Here comes Suz from Missoula, Montana, passing the mile twenty-two aid station!" He'd be jogging alongside me now, helping remove my running vest so he can refill my water, "Hhhaahhhh! Hhahh! Only nine miles to go to finish 50K! Let's hear it for Suz!"

I high five a tree branch, imagining it's John. Closing my eyes, I try to feel the way he would smack my ass as I head on. After a moment I smack it myself, but somehow it's not the same.

Refocusing on the present, I glance behind me and consider the intelligence of continuing past the cabin. I am alarmingly low on water. Finding the cabin would allow me to restock and reset, grab the rest of my gear, prepare a little better for what is clearly a longer rescue mission than anticipated. Maybe John's even there! If not John, maybe Alfred or someone else who could help. I could even search the cabin for maps. An emergency radio!

Feeling good about this logic, but angry to backtrack, I grab the pack and turn around again, trudging along the way I came.

This time I'm walking, "No more mistakes, Suz. This is getting dangerous."

Approaching evening. No cabin! Four more miles backtracking, twenty-six total now! Again extra miles past where it should be, to be safe, make sure I didn't miss anything. The endlessly smooth, easy trail, lined by trees. Mind numbing.

Hands on my hips, "This is crazy. What the flying fuck?"

A chipmunk scurries up the tree next to me, stopping a few feet above my head, peering down.

"Hello kind sir. Do you have a friend or cousin who lives next to a cabin? Do you have his address perchance? I'm in a bit of a bind." He scurries on up the tree. Jerk.

I close my eyes, thinking it through. I was painstakingly slow after turning around this afternoon, carefully scanning the woods on my left the entire time, absolutely guaranteeing I not miss the cabin trail again. The only explanation is I didn't go far enough before turning around. My GPS watch must be way off under this tree cover, another rookie mistake! The cabin has got to be behind me. Scowling a bit, I sigh. I'm skeptical, but this is the only reasonable explanation. It has to be true.

Deciding I'll be spending the night in the woods again, I remember a small flat spot just off trail a few minutes back. As I don't want to catch any more flesh-eating fungus, an actual spot to lay my sleeping bag before dark sounds amazing. Settled on a plan, I feel buoyed slightly.

Turning around, I nod decisively, try to smile. I slap the chipmunk's tree, hoping to scare him, which helps a little. I walk.

Making a bed of pine needles in the flat spot, I crawl into my sleeping bag for the night, staring blankly up at the tree canopy. The upper reaches sway slightly in a twilight breeze, briefly transporting me back to the old oak. I catch my breath but can't hold onto the feeling. This is different. Sinister.

I'm terribly thirsty, having seen no creeks. I drank most of my water jogging back to the cabin, but still hit mile twenty severely dehydrated. When I couldn't find the trail I started rationing the remains, but now I'm down to mere sips. I'm hungry too, with only a little mango left, but this feels unimportant next to the burning thirst.

Fuck this place! I don't know where I am, and I can't find the single landmark I know is out in these endless trees!

Looking around I take a deep breath and admit I am lost. Without a water source, I could die out here.

I sit up and begin to cry. Not my usual, stoic, expressionless stare with tears leaking out, but an outright snotty, whimpering, shuddering, full bodied bawl. It's an epic cry of the sort I've not had since I crushed Jasper's motorcycle.

Increasingly it feels cathartic. I'm no longer crying because I am lost and scared, I'm crying for my nine-year-old tribe, for Rachel and Ethan, sunlit fields, shady oaks, and everything I gave up. Because I was too scared to love, too scared of the vulnerability in apologizing. They would have forgiven without hesitation! But it would have required admitting I loved them too, and this was simply not possible. I chose alone and safe within myself instead. I'm crying for Jasper, his insecurity and pride, not being able to forgive my mother, taking it out on me. I was ten you bastard! I'm crying for John never hearing that I love him. This notion makes me moan quietly, feeling the most immediately tragic.

"I love you." I whisper. Then louder, "John, I love you!" Rolling off the tongue more easily now, "I love you." Stated as fact, feeling the most real.

"Goddamnit! Where the fuck are you? Where the fuck am I?" Throwing a pile of pine needles at nothing.

"I'm sorry I thought of you as an unchallenging taco! You challenge me every day, patiently waiting for me to admit my feelings, inspiring me to explore them, encouraging me to be a better person, taking me on longer and longer runs, making life an everyday adventure! I'm sorry I make fun of the way you elucidate about the world around you. I love your big brain! John, I love YOU."

Feeling a great weight off my shoulders, I yell, "You do have a magic penis! Expecto Orgasmiasmo!" Laying back in the pine needles with a huff.

Exhausted and emotionally spent, I sleep. In the middle of nowhere, lost, confused, frightened, I sleep better than I have in years.

7

Dawn. Again. I mentally tally 'Day Two', like I'm some kind of convict, keeping track of days. Or is it 'Day Three?' Do I count the evening I left the cabin as 'One?' Remarkably, that was the first day at the cabin. A lot has happened since then. I'm counting it.

"Day Three," I nod to the largest tree nearby, "In case you're wondering."

I pack up my sleeping bag, eat the last of my Mango, savor one tiny sip of water. I walk back towards the cabin. I hope towards the cabin anyway.

Mid-afternoon. My watch battery died hours ago at mile thirty-one, as if it didn't care beyond a 50K. I know I've passed where the cabin should be, but no longer care. There were no side trails. I am far too tired to even consider turning around again. I tell myself John couldn't find the cabin either and is ahead somewhere.

Having finished the last bit of water this morning, I'm worried I'll become delusional with dehydration. I've heard

crazy stories from ultra-running friends, some of the wild
things they've imagined late in a long race.

I'd leave the trail if I heard a stream, which scares me all
the more. Never leave the trail when you're lost! I'm
speculating on the odds of dying out here. If I can find water,
I've got time. Without water? I shake my head.

Even if I don't find John I have to keep going this way. This
trail must lead somewhere. I know there's no water behind
me. If I have to help myself before helping him, that's just the
way it is.

Sneering at the trail, I curse my memory once more. I don't
even know how long we told anyone we'd be out
backpacking. How long will it be until someone realizes we're
missing? Should I stay by a stream and wait to be found?
Guess I'll worry about that when I find one.

Late afternoon. Another evening in the woods
approaching. I'm dizzy, my exhaustion hanging about me like
a cloud. One step at a time.

Coming around a corner, the forest falls away, revealing a
rocky outcropping next to a cliff. I cheer at the change in
scenery, doing a weak little skip.

"I'll be," I mumble, shaking the cloud away, slapping my
cheeks a few times.

Following the tree line around the bend, I gasp lightly.
Frozen, I tear up. The trail continues along the cliff! The sort
that always make me nervous to run, but John plows through,
confident on his feet.

Trying to shake the fear away, I hurry over, noticing it's
where Rachel's doppelganger stood in the picture. It's steeply
sloped for maybe ten feet, but not so steep as to see directly
down.

Desperately I yell for John a few times. "John?! Jooohhnn!
Holy fuck! JOOOHHNN?!" Silence. A breeze ruffles my hair
in response. The indifference all around chokes me, and I fight

an urge to curl up right there on the trail, fetal position, and give up.

I'm shaking despite the afternoon sun. Dehydration, hunger, fear threaten to swallow me, held at bay only by an anger burning in my chest. How could I let this happen? Why doesn't anyone care? How could you do this to me? I'm not certain who 'you' is. I want to scream, but can't survive another swift return of oppressive silence.

Gripping a tree behind me, I feel slightly grounded. Breathe. I rein in the cacophony of emotions, try to settle. Breathe.

Uncertain on my next step, I stare blankly at the view. Rolling hills, green with nothing but trees. Distant, larger mountains. Doesn't look like the Rockies though. Oregon, I think, maybe Washington.

Refocusing, I look down, miserable with the task at hand. The slope to the cliff is mostly slippery sand and loose rocks, no vegetation for stability, ancient lava probably. Absently, I think Oregon.

I take one tentative step, sliding immediately, pulling my foot back. Laying down on my belly for maximum traction, I breathe deep and slither downhill towards the cliff's edge, still sliding slightly, my heart pounding in my ears!

Peering over, gripping the edge as best I can, the drop is abrupt and terrifying! Squinting, I don't see anything that looks like a person. No flashes of color, no obvious broken tree branches on the way down. For a long moment I lay my cheek in the scree, tears coloring the dry rocks I'm so relieved I didn't just find his shattered body.

Looking again, I can't make out the trees at the bottom. Got to be a few thousand feet, maybe more. If he went over the edge with momentum, clearing the closer spattering of trees... I swallow hard, trying to hold down the bile abruptly burning the back of my throat.

I lay there for an eternity, trying to assure myself he's not at the bottom. Developing a headache from laying downhill, my feet so much higher than my head, I finally nod decisively. Not there. Probably never even passed this way.

It's getting late and I need to camp, the rocky outcropping before the cliff a nice spot. Will certainly have starlight here, likely even a moon sliver by now.

Carefully, awkwardly, sliding here and there, I turn around on my belly and slither back up to the trail, standing once I'm back on solid ground.

I let out a tremendous sigh of relief, deflating like a balloon, hands on my head, shaking like a leaf with spent adrenaline. Startled, I see there's a chipmunk sitting on his haunches in the trail.

Dropping my arms, I try to smile. "Well hello little guy."

Looking back out at the mountains, I shake my head, "Whew. I do not like heights my friend," he doesn't move, cocking his head at me, holding a nut.

"Ok, go on along, I'm going to camp over there behind you. See my pack?"

Suddenly he stands straight up on his feet, throwing his paws in the air and flinging the nut about ten inches to his left. He's chittering at me like a madman, and striding towards me, upright.

Shocked, I take a step back. I step with my inside foot, away from the cliff, a primitive safety measure my brain instinctively enforces.

The trail curves behind me though. My foot hits loose rock, inches from solid ground.

Dimly, as I totter off balance, inside foot sliding wildly, outside foot too weak to compensate as I fall, I register he looks like a miniature grizzly bear, standing tall with his arms up like that.

Then my hip, immediately followed by my shoulder and face, smack the slope. My brain empties. I leave my stomach with the chipmunk. I flail!

My forearm collides with something solid, a lightning bolt of pain, then numbness below the elbow. In a surreal moment, I feel as though I went running and fell off a cliffside trail, fulfilling a fear I've had since I took up trail running.

I went skydiving with John once, purportedly to conquer my fear of heights. Remarkably it was fun, and I loved his enthusiasm. I close my eyes and channel that feeling. It's comforting. Instead of panic I feel a sort of calm. I relax my arms and think about that Björk song, the one where she flings herself from a cliff and wonders if her eyes will be closed or open when they find her.

I squinch my eyes closed as tightly as I can. A blankly staring corpse is so creepy.

PART II

So we beat on, boats against the current,
borne back ceaselessly into the past.

The Great Gatsby, F. Scott Fitzgerald

1

Breathe.

I glance about to find myself in a rickety cabin I explored as a child. Awash with memory, I can feel the magic and mystery invoked by that bright-eyed little girl. It was all around as I tentatively tiptoed, a treasure waiting in every closet, behind every book, under a secret floorboard. Today I stand stock still, an emotional chill leaving goosebumps in its wake. Instantly familiar, yet out of place in time, the warm sunlight sparkling on the dust I've stirred. I inhale the stale, amber atmosphere. My breath catches. For a moment the walls act strangely, arching towards the depth of my morning yawn. No. Making the sound of a dying seagull, "bhrugurhubrhu!" I shake the sleep away. Is that the sound a dying seagull makes? I've never been here. Where the hell am I even? Surreal. Where's the F-ing coffee?

I can smell it. I wander into the kitchen to find a cup waiting for me, steaming. Man alive I love having a cup of coffee ready for me. A porch swing is creaking outside so I walk on out.

Ethan's sitting there with his cup, having a stare down with a robin on the railing of the deck. They both smile up at me, well, the robin only looks, but I imagine it smiling. Ethan pats the spot next to him.

"Look at this guy. He's been sitting here with me for the last few minutes. Sometimes staring right at me! Mostly just hopping around though, man is he cute." Beaming at me, he laughs. "This place is amazing. You're amazing. I'm glad the coffee smell got you up while it was still hot."

Looking at Ethan sitting there, for a moment something feels very wrong, but I can't place it. I stare at him with the disorienting sensation that he should be taller, more muscular, with darker hair and a light beard. I'm ashamed as I realize this is an apt description of the sort of guys I dated before him, likely a guilty byproduct of whatever I dreamed last night. Fuck Freud and his wish fulfillment!

Of course it's the same ol' Ethan. Light brown, wavy hair trying to escape in all directions, always falling into his face, long enough to tuck behind his ears but usually held back with a headband or clips. Both ears pierced with grey hoops, and black, thick rimmed glasses highlighting gold tinted, hazel eyes that always sparkle happily. He's too skinny in a toned, broad shoulder, narrow waist sort of way, having swum competitively through college. His shirts tend to sag shapelessly on him like he's some kind of oddly formed hanger, and I'm always surprised to find sharply defined muscles underneath whenever he takes one off. He still logs countless laps in the pool, often the entire time I'm out on long runs, and eats more than can possibly be healthy. Despite the mismatch with my historical boyfriend catalog, I am universally comforted by his single most defining characteristic, which persists from childhood despite losing his baby fat face to athletically angular cheekbones. The way his goofy smile impossibly takes up his entire face! It's remarkably endearing and ever present.

I sit down next to him and nuzzle into his side, flinging my legs across his lap.

"Thanks for making my coffee, E."

"Of course. How are you feeling? You seemed a little off last night."

I don't remember last night. I don't remember how we got to this cabin. Taking a sip of the coffee I try to sort out my thoughts. "I'm fine. Worn out I think. Thanks."

He looks at me for a second, knowing I'm not offering the whole truth. He doesn't push it of course. Ethan reads me like a favorite book. Knows what I need. Who I am. Mostly I love the comfort of being with someone where so much goes unspoken, but it's definitely a double-edged sword. Sometimes I feel I don't have any private thoughts at all.

Placing my hand on his chest, "How did we get here?"

"What do you mean? You don't remember finding the trail?"

I shake my head, looking up at him.

"You spotted a side trail with an odd sign." Jabbing the air with each word for emphasis, "Deus! Ex! Machina!" lower, imitating an echo, "machina, machina, machina."

He pauses, smiling at me, "I wanted to keep going, lots of ground to cover, but you got pretty excited about that sign, so we checked it out. Nearly a bushwhack down the trail, but here we are, another Susan win! Look at this place!"

The trees seem to shimmer impossibly, like a wave. The robin on the railing watches me. I close my eyes, trying to wake up, "Deus Ex Machina? Bizarre."

"Heh, yeah. What did you say it means again?"

I open my eyes and the robin is still staring, "God from the Machine. It's a literary term."

"Mm. Like when God rolled into the synagogue in his tank, popping out of the hatch, long white hair and beard blowing in the wind, spraying his machine gun into the ceiling. Eh eh eh eh eh eh eh eh! Roof tiles falling, people screaming. He stops firing and yells, 'Get the hell out of my house you scoundrels!' A brief pause, then pandemonium as all the merchants and traders stream for the door. Right?"

Laughing, I grab a pillow to put against the armrest so I can lean back and look at him more directly, smacking him with it first, "Yes that's exactly right. Why did his beard blow in the wind inside the synagogue?"

"Synagogues. Drafty places. Besides he's god. If I had an epic white beard and could make it blow whenever I wanted, you're god damn right I would."

Losing the smile, he furrows his brow a little, a look I know means he's debating the merits of pursuing a subject, "Why don't you remember the trail?"

I shrug, "I don't know. Actually I don't remember hiking here at all. The last thing I remember is getting ready for a run, and even that feels vague."

He sits up straighter, now legitimately concerned, "A run? We didn't hike here, we backpacked here, thirty-one miles, four days!"

This shakes me up. Putting the coffee cup on the deck to avoid a spill, "Four days. You're shitting me."

"I shit you not."

We sit silently a minute, Ethan settling back into the swing. "Did you bump your head?"

Smiling a little, "Ah, well maybe I don't remember that either? I don't feel a knot anywhere."

He echoes my sorta smile, "I'm not sure what to make of that. Maybe we should get you to a doctor. CT scan or something. Let's keep an eye out for any other neurological symptoms. Hasn't happened before has it?"

"I don't think so. I suppose little ones might go unnoticed, but not an actual time gap like this, no."

A chipmunk is on the deck now too, next to my coffee cup, cradling a nut in his paw. Breaks the tension. Ethan stops the swing with his toes, trying not to scare him. I pick my cup back up gently, taking it away from the overly interested chipmunk.

He smiles, "Well hello there little buddy, got a nice juicy nut for breakfast? Want to have it with some coffee?"

Looking back at me, Ethan strokes my head a couple of times, brushing my hair aside, running his hand through it. "You're not allowed to have a brain tumor lover, you're too much a part of me."

Pulling his hand out of my hair, I kiss his fingers. It is hard to imagine my life without Ethan, having been companions since we were seven, and I know it would be so much worse for him. The second I have this thought it startles me a bit, the clear admission that he is more attached. Or is it more committed? More in love? I frown for a moment before brushing it all away. He's like a brother to me. I hope he didn't catch the frown.

"I'm sure it's fine. Can't overwork cause amnesia? I've been killing myself over my book, training for the ultra, not resting enough. You take me out into the woods where there's nothing to do but rest and relax, boom! my brain says, 'thank fucking Christ,' and turns off."

"Only you would define backpacking thirty plus miles as resting, but yeah, maybe that's plausible. I'm sure it's something simple like that." He scratches his neck, then rests his hand on my leg, giving it a little reassuring squeeze, for himself as much as me.

We stare off into the woods in a companionable silence. Ethan rocks the swing lightly, causing a quiet creak. I sigh, confused but content. The chipmunk is chittering, and he actually throws the nut.

2

Ethan is my rock when I need to unwind. Even as children he would calm me down, soothe my nerves, dig a smile out of me. Around eight or nine he started carrying around peppermints, my favorite candy, so he'd have them on hand for emergencies. I distinctly remember the first time, crying under our old oak, something my big sister Alice had said. He popped up and started dancing, a respectable imitation of my usual antics, Rachel already laughing. Then he starts providing a little theme music, 'Bum, ba-dum, dum! Bum, ba-dum, dum, dum!' waving his arms around, suddenly producing a peppermint. He presents it to me, down on one knee with his head bowed, passionately yelling 'My Queen!' Tears completely forgotten, I was speechless. Then the big goofy grin, tossing another one to Rachel, popping one of his own, flopping back down between us. I'm smiling broadly too, his eyes sparkling with pride, Rachel happily humming some derivation of the theme music to a passing dragonfly.

Now, twenty odd years later, he's an attentive and observant boyfriend, and I often marvel at how any girl would consider themselves lucky. He's worried about my brain today though, and encouraging me to stay put. He made lunch, a black bean soup he dehydrated last week, serving it along with naan to scoop it up. His attention is often too much, but I'm happy to oblige him right now. Hardly moving from the swing, dozing off and on, I'm hoping my memory will clear.

Munching his naan, Ethan turns to me, "Whoever lives here must feed these guys, they're way too comfortable with us. They're even too comfortable with each other. It's weird."

The chipmunk is up on the railing now, looking at us, the robin only a foot or so away, beak nestled into its wing, looking asleep.

"Speaking of who lives here, aren't we trespassing? Do you know anything about the owner?"

He shrugs, "Maybe. I dunno, Deus Ex Machina right? Did you see the sign over the door?"

I lean backwards, Ethan holding my legs to give me leverage.

You Are Here
All Who Seek
All Who Wander
-- And Wonder --
You Are Welcome

He's reading it too, "I'm all three of those things, and I'm here, so I guess I'm welcome. We're in the middle of nowhere yet the place seems to be stocked for guests, plenty of clean sheets and towels. Vibrator charged in the bedside table."

I dribble some black beans down my chin, giggling, "A little too accommodating don't you think?" I love how Ethan makes me laugh.

He smiles, "Actually there's no power. Hot water though. Propane tank around back."

Backing up to my original question, "Nothing about the owner though?"

Ethan shakes his head, "Not that I've found. I've named him Alfred."

"Naturally. Why Alfred?"

"Well, you know, Batman's butler." As if this explains it. My silence prompts him to continue. He shrugs, "Alfred knows all about the Batcave, but it's no big deal to him, just one more place to butle. And he's one hell of a butler to batman, making sure everything's taken care of in the mansion and the cave at all times. Keeping batman's secrets without question, second nature. So what does a guy like that do in his free time? He loves butling, right? Serving people, making things run smoothly, but not just for anybody, only amazing people like batman. Plus it's stressful work, your employer, basically a son, constantly risking life and limb, beaten and bruised all the time. Alfred needs somewhere to unwind, his own miniature version of the Batcave! He comes up with the idea for this cabin. Something hidden, but slick, functional, attracting the right kind of people down a near invisible trail when he's away, busy keeping batman alive. And who would take that trail unless they appreciate seeing Deus Ex Machina in the woods?" Gesturing at me in a little half salute, half bow, "Then they get here, see the door sign, and know they're home. Alfred's work is done."

He pauses, smiling, "There's probably some little bell dinging in the Batcave, so he'll know to come change the sheets and clean up after we leave."

I smile at Ethan, still seeing the excited, imaginative little boy I knew. Leaning forward I kiss him on the nose, "Who knew Alfred was a secret woodsman?" clinking my bowl against his, "Makes sense to me. Cheers."

I lean back onto the cushion, breathing deep. It does sound like something I would come up with, given a little more time. Alfred fits.

3

Kissing Ethan on the nose definitely gave him ideas, that soft look swimming in his eyes. I have to pop up to avoid it.

"I need a shower my friend."

He frowns lightly, registering this small rejection, but doesn't acknowledge it. "Sounds good, I'll be out here with the locals. By time you get back I'll have this chipmunk rocking with me on the swing!"

The bathroom is lovely, a dusty skylight illuminating plenty of towels and an opulent white rug. I step gingerly, given my dirty feet, surprised to find it damp. I clearly haven't showered, so Ethan must have taken one last night. He didn't look like it though. The hot water etches rivulets down the grime on my legs. It. Is. Glorious!

Sex with Ethan is fine. More than fine. He approaches it the same way he does our relationship. Patient, always waiting for me to finish, sweet. Connecting. It's just not, ah, animalistic! I want to be fully lost in it, unable to think straight, a toe curling, world obliterating, mind numbing, decadent experience, empty of time. Forced into the now, nothing but my body. No, not my body, nothing but me. Oliver! I actually place my hand on my chest, catching my breath.

"Heh, Suz you're a fool," I chuckle to myself.

What a terrible relationship that was! I'm sixteen, Oliver twenty, the age gap feeling more horrible in retrospect. But he taught me to come, and repeatedly, opening up a brave new world. Zero ambition, not that bright, working the evening shift in some warehouse, Oliver would spend eight hours a day unloading pallets, stacking boxes. He was built, and coming back to his apartment around midnight, still damp from the mind-numbing, blood pumping trial of muscular endurance, he'd find me there, naked and mischievous, wanting him before he showered. I loved the way he smelled, Pavlovian.

We met at the Hive, a bar in town where the running joke was a note from your mother got you served, 'My little girl is 21, I promise. Hugs!'

Rachel and I snuck out to meet there, flex a little teenage-independence muscle. He was there after work with some friends, and standing next to him to get my IPA I was transfixed!

Certainly he was hot, but it was the light, clean musk he gave off! A moth to the flame. It was the first time I associated my burgeoning sexuality with an animalistic response, and I was already lost in the feeling. Told him I was nineteen. Went home with him that night.

Remarkably, I spent the next six months sneaking out four or five nights a week before I got caught. I don't think Oliver ever knew my birthday, favorite color, book, didn't care. Actually shrugged when I confessed I was in high school. Not the jackhammer type, he'd go down on me, maybe grind me into the bed for a while, sweaty, powerful and slow, later teaching me to take charge. Every time I'm nothing but hormones, blind passion. Then we'd fall asleep, my alarm set for four, home by four-fifteen to sneak back in. I slept though classes, couldn't think straight, the next night not soon enough. A full-on addict.

Would solve a lot of problems if they could bottle Oliver's pheromones. Closing my eyes, I have this vision of a sparkling, ornate blue vial in the bedside table. Ethan's reading on his side, his back to me, I sprinkle a little on him. Turning over he asks, 'What was that?' 'Nothing you sexy beast, get over here and take me!'

Revved up with the memory, I wish Alfred really did provide a vibrator, sneak in a quick one. Course Ethan would happily take the role, but I can't use him that way, not with the ghost of Oliver swirling around.

Tugging my armpit hair, I laugh. It's a kind of bizarre karma that I end up with Ethan, someone who's absolutely intoxicated with my pheromones.

Smiling, I remember how sheepish he looked, confessing he thought it'd be hot if I stopped shaving. "It might be sexy lover. That's what armpit hair is for, wicking sweat away from the skin, distributing your pheromones before the bacteria makes it go sour with actual body odor." Shrugging, averting his eyes a little, "Just a thought. I don't want you to feel uncomfortable."

Always the rebel, game to be different, I stopped that day. Got some weird looks. After a month I was ready to throw in the towel on the societal experiment, when a male yoga teacher pulled me aside after class to discuss my hygiene. Apparently I'm a distraction to his students.

Infuriated, I lift my arm in his face, demanding, "Do I stink? Do you shave your armpits?" Knowing he didn't. Emphatically pointing at the front door, "How many men walk through that door with hairy armpits? Eighty percent?"

People are packing up their mats, and I'm making a scene. He frowns at me, angry, but saying nothing. After a moment he turns around, walking off. Everyone is looking at me, not looking at the same time, hyperaware.

Given the audience, I lift both arms up, smelling the right, nodding with satisfaction. "I smell fucking amazing," I declare to no one in particular.

Generally avoiding his class, but making sure to show up enough for my pride, a month or so later I walk in, seeing two girls in back giggling when they spot me. I don't understand this until the first sun salutations.

Laughing, I make eye contact with our slightly scowling instructor. A fine show of female solidarity indeed. After class they come over to my mat excitedly.

Smiling broadly, one whispers, "I'm so glad we finally saw you, I'm going home to shave right now." She flutters a little, breathless, "But that day was amazing, we had to do it!"

The other girl chuckles, "I'm not. I love it. Girl power!"

Bemused, I watch them wave at the instructor on the way out, arms held high. To this day I only shave for special events, thanks to him.

Still toying with the hair, running my thumb through my armpit, I'm momentarily disconnected from reality, the feeling of recently shaved stubble prickling. Feeling dizzy, disoriented, I sink down and sit in the shower, letting the warm spray massage my neck.

Oddly, bracing myself on the lip of the tub to sit shot a sharp, dramatic pain through my forearm, making me gasp. The bathroom seems to tilt. Dimly, I tug my armpit hair again, no stubble there of course. I haven't shaved since when? Ryan and Stephanie's wedding? Close to two years I think.

Shaking my head, letting out a long breath, the room stabilizes. "Brain, what are you doing? What is this?"

4

Dressed. Refreshed. I'm blotting my hair with one of Alfred's pink towels, walking into the living room, and I see Ethan standing stock still in the middle of the rug, staring, one hand raised slightly.

Noticing me, he snaps out of it, gesturing me over. Guiding me, hands on both shoulders, he places me in his spot, facing the bookshelf.

"What do you see?"

Seeing the picture across the room, "Holy shit, is that Rachel?"

Walking over he picks it up, saying quietly, "I thought so too at first. It's not though of course. How creepy would that be?" A beat passes, "The guy next to her looks like John, dude from my English class."

"Mm," I say, still staring at the almost Rachel. "Who's John?"

Ethan smiles a little, "Just the guy we owe our relationship to. He inspired me to take the plunge and pursue you. Only reason I remember him."

I look closer at the picture, "He's hot, I kinda want to chew on his legs a little. Maybe we can thank him with a threesome?"

Ethan laughs, "Ah, I love it when you lust after other men." Tapping the guy in the picture, "No, he came up to me at a party, asking about you. Had seen us together, wanted to know if you were single, if he might be your type, etc. Good looking guy like that, fit, one of the smartest in class, always writing these heart-rending short stories. I figured it was a matter of time. I went home right away, slightly drunk and shaking," He shrugs, "I couldn't let it happen. Started planning my big move that night."

Trying to look incredulous, "You kept me from those calves? I'd have traded Samson for one night!" A flash of hurt in his eyes, I've gone too far. Pushing him playfully, "You know I'm kidding."

I try to steer the subject to safer ground, "Samson would have loved it here, terrifying that chipmunk. Damn that piece of shit invisible fence!"

We're quiet a moment, both lost in Samson's conjured presence, and I suppress a wave of guilt in being flippant about him. Smiling lightly, I nudge Ethan again, "I can't imagine the patience you had with that puppy."

Relieved, I watch the casual happiness seep back into his eyes. He laughs, putting the picture back in place. "I had everything to gain. I didn't even go to class for almost two weeks, terrified John would do something. Took a lot of treats to keep Samson from shaking the roses all over the place, or chewing the straps. I made him wear it until he ignored it. He was a smart pup though." He beams at me.

I lean against his chest, remembering. It was a phenomenal gesture. Storybook. My parents never let me have a dog, so Ethan adopts this three-week-old lab at the local shelter.

Designs a kind of sling, leather, sews it himself, and trains the puppy using a bunch of pencils in it.

Finally ready, he cuts half a dozen roses down to six inches and secures them in the sling like a quiver of arrows, taping a tiny letter behind the quiver. Has a helium balloon custom designed, a leafy tree dominating the balloon, sketched in white against a red background, the branches arching over my name in big block letters. Tying it to Samson's collar, he lets the puppy loose into my dorm one fateful Saturday morning. Pandemonium ensues. Ethan waits outside on a park bench, casually, both arms resting on the back. It doesn't take long.

Suddenly there's banging on my dorm room door. I open it, shocked to find nothing short of fifteen giggling girls, laughing, all trying to see my face. They part, letting Samson dance into the room, the balloon bobbing wildly. One of them hands me the tiny note, having fallen from the quiver in Samson's excitement.

Hi! My name is Samson!
Ethan tells me I'll live at his apartment,
but I'm really yours.
I'm so excited to meet you,
and I hope you visit every single day!

A little paw print underneath, and then below that, tears leaking down my face, I read,

I've loved you for fourteen years.
You're my best friend.
And I'll spend the rest of my life by your side,
trying to make you as happy as you feel right now.
Let's be what we're meant to be.
Yours,
Ethan

Silently I hand the letter to someone and it's quickly passed around. The room's quiet, except Samson's snuffling at my laundry and a few girls crying. I look up, taking it in, some with a hand on their chest, or lightly covering their mouths, others with eyes closed, swaying, fantasies flowing, romantic visions flickering across their faces, vicarious.

I wipe the tears away, mouth half open, staring at everyone, dumbfounded. The decision is easy of course, in the last eight years I've never really questioned dating him. I don't feel the girlish excitement that saturates the room, but I feel safe. I cuddle Samson, wondering what my new future will be like.

Ethan's quiet, knowing I'm reliving it. As always, the memory frees a tear, and he catches it on his finger.

"You could have dated any girl in my entire dorm."

He smiles, "Only wanted one."

5

Feeling drained, I throw myself onto the couch, patting the cushion next to me. Smiling, I ask him, "Do you still keep up with Rachel?"

The lighting in the room dims, a cloud sliding by outside. A moment passes and I notice Ethan is glaring at me, but then the glare turns to concern. Kneeling next to me he takes my hand, whispering, "What the fuck is wrong with you Susan?"

I can't reconcile this statement at first, but I draw in a shocked breath as a curtain flicks open in my brain. Of course. Rachel is dead. Killed herself senior year of high school. I don't know what to say.

Climbing onto the couch with me, he puts his head in his hands. "I still blame myself you know."

"I've never understood that." Stroking his cheek, "Sure, we should have been there for her, but she made her choices. Went down a pretty dark path. You can't shoulder all the blame."

He looks up at me, eyes wet, morose. "You're right I guess. I've never told you the whole story though. Didn't want to burden you with it. It's bad."

Taken aback, I rest my hand in my lap. I didn't think Ethan kept anything from me. "Well, now's as good a time as any, here with her doppelganger."

I push myself up, grab the picture and hand it to him, "Alfred would want you to unburden, here in his magic cabin."

He smiles lightly at me, "It was a long time ago Susan. Let sleeping dogs lie, as they say."

I sit back down, closer to him, threading my arm through his, and wait. I can tell he's in that space.

He sighs, sitting back, sliding his hand into mine, interlacing our fingers. "Well, everything went to shit right after she put the moves on you. Straight downhill."

I color at this memory. I know they talked about it, and he and I have too, in vague terms, but it's still an uncomfortable space.

He looks at me, amused by my blush, "I encouraged her you know, helped her design that whole scene, actually played your part in it over and over again, while she practiced."

I didn't know this. I can definitely see it, and I smile at the idea of Rachel holding Ethan that way. I wonder how far they took the scene exactly, but the mood's not right to ask. File that question away for later.

"Male pride, after you rejected me I thought maybe you really were gay. Partly, I wanted you both to be happy, but I also simply wanted to see you date a girl. Would have made me feel infinitely better. Course I didn't know about Oliver until we were adults. She never mentioned him, probably to spare me, but now that I know I can't imagine how she convinced herself you weren't straight. She said you didn't know what you were. Hope springs eternal I guess."

I squeeze his hand, not liking Oliver's name in the story, feeling more guilty having so recently thought of him.

I redirect, "So you set her up to fail. That hardly means you drove her to," I pause, not wanting to say it out loud, "to do the things she did later."

"It's not that, it's the fact that I wasn't there for her after. She was broken hearted, and I aggressively defended you instead of comforting her, instead of being the friend she really needed. I was angry. I felt she'd proven you weren't gay, and your rejection of me felt all the more poignant, hitting me all at once, all over again."

Getting upset with himself, raising his voice a little, "On the other hand, despite not seeing much of you after we had sex, I still loved you. I was mad she'd pushed you to react the way you did. Said she was foolish. She should have stopped earlier. Shouldn't have made you so uncomfortable. Blah, blah, blah. I was yelling."

Pausing, he blows out a breath, "I left her under the oak, stomping off in a hurry, not able to look at her."

Coughing lightly, he scratches his neck, uncomfortable. Squinting at the fireplace, he pushes on, "She chased me down, hit me like a hammer right in the middle of my back, closed fist, left a terrific bruise. I turned and actually stumbled backwards at the sight of her."

He shakes his head, quieter now, "I still see that face, tears streaked everywhere, snot unwiped, running sideways to her cheek, but absolutely smoldering. I have never seen such rage. Why didn't I come to my senses right then?"

Placing my other hand on top of ours, I wait.

"Hoarsely she hissed at me, 'You're telling me I've lost my two best friends at once.' I stared a moment, actually frightened of her. I straightened up. I said yes and," he pauses, "and I walked off. Total silence behind me." Almost a whisper now, "I've never been back to that old oak."

He lets out a long, heavy breath, deflating like a balloon. The air in the room is unbearably heavy, stifling. Ethan grunts and shakes his head. "We didn't speak for a year."

My eyes are busy leaking again, thinking of Rachel's fury and pain. Noticing, Ethan leans against my shoulder, mumbles, "It gets worse."

He's quiet, waiting to see if I want him to go on. I'm not sure I do, but at this point I have to know, "What happened?"

Looking at me, "I know you heard all the rumors. Parties, drinking, drugs, sex, failing out of school?"

I nod. Everyone did. I'd heard she got a couple of STDs. Dated a thirty-something biker chick. Went on a bender in Mexico. She was a favorite source of high school gossip, and wild rumors circulated. I doubted most of them, and still do, but she definitely failed out. That was true.

Closing his eyes now, "Well, it all started the night I left her, after we both rejected her. She decided to make the scene true. Sorta. Went to a basketball party. Got hammered and came on to that guy Steve. Nothing like the Steve she had invented of course. He took her into a bedroom, a bit rough, maybe five minutes. Left yelling triumphantly at his friends the moment he opened the door, her laying there half naked, semi-conscious. She passed out and woke up to four or five of them."

Now Ethan is crying softly, something I don't have much experience with. Almost inaudibly he mutters, "They passed her around Susan."

I might be sick. Now I know exactly how Ethan is feeling. I should have been there for her too! How petty I was! Oh my god.

He sits up straight, wiping his eyes and nose, embarrassed. I pat him awkwardly, trying to reassure that it's ok to cry.

Shying away from my hand, he takes it in his instead. "She called me on the anniversary of that night, a year after I abandoned her at the oak. She'd taken a bottle of her dad's pain killers, told me the whole story, and in horrifying detail, while I rushed over to her house. I didn't want to know, but I kept asking more and more about it, trying to keep her awake on the phone. I had called 911 from my parent's land line first, struggling through two conversations at once, but still beat the ambulance by a solid five minutes. Longest five minutes of my life. When I got there I kept her awake every way I could. An eternity later the ambulance arrived and they pumped her stomach, took her in. She ended up in a psych ward for three days."

I can't believe I've never heard any of these details. Where was I? Late senior year, I'd have been fooling around with that asshole Patrick. Probably making out in his truck the very moment Ethan's busy saving Rachel's life. If I'd made more effort with either of them, instead of hiding away in meaningless relationships, I would have been there too. I'm staring at the fireplace, mute.

Ethan sighs again, "I tried to reconnect after that, be there for her, but she didn't remember any of that night. We hung out a little, but it was awkward at best. She was always distant, often going silent in the middle of a conversation, not really with me."

He follows my eyes to the fireplace. "Didn't call me the next time."

He stands up, lightly brushing his chest like he walked into a spider web, trying to wipe the story away. Looking down at me, hands in his pockets now, "Left me a note though. Her mom hand delivered it a few weeks later. She didn't say anything, just stood in the doorway crying, the envelope still sealed with my name on it. I can't imagine that debate, desperate to know what it said, torn with honoring your dead daughter's privacy. I gave it back to her later that week. Took pictures of it for my computer first of course. Used to read it every year on the anniversary."

I look up at him, my heart in my throat, dreading Rachel's final thoughts.

Starting in a monotone, but quickly picking up a smile, "It was lovely. She reminisced about our spot under the oak, the light dancing through the leaves, the creek, our fort. Mentioned the way I used to hold her, your constant dances. It was a flowing, flowery, multi-page stream of consciousness about our childhoods, mostly taking place right there in that field. Said she didn't understand why it got so complicated, or when, and that she missed us both. Wanted me to know it wasn't my fault, or yours. Thanked me for being there for her, before she fell off the deep end, and for being her best friend. The only thing she wanted was for me to reconnect with you, so we could be there for each other through 'the challenges of life.' That was her phrase. Used it repeatedly."

He takes a deep breath, staring out the window behind me. "I remember the ending word for word I think. Every time I braved rereading it, I'd get stuck reading the end over and over." Closing his eyes, he recites, "'Ethan, please reach out to Suzy. You must reconnect! You will need each other through the challenges of life, as I needed both of you but had too much pride to ask. I have been so lost! And I simply can't let that happen to either of you. Lay down your pride and be there for each other. Be the best friends we've always been. I know this letter will make you do it. The idea fills me with happiness! I am done Ethan. I accept that. It's ok. But it's not too late for either of you, together. Please don't let it slip away. I think of our laughter, Suzy doing some silly dance, spinning, your goofy smile, and I hold it to my chest until I'm full. I just took the pills. Soon I'll be free.'"

Pausing for a moment, overwhelmed, he takes another breath and plows forward, looking directly at me again. "Further down the last page, she wrote, 'It's been half an hour, I thought about calling, but I'm ready. My heart is still full. Thank you.' And at the very bottom, in large, shaky letters, she scribbled, 'I love you both, I always have, I always will.'"

I sit up and begin to cry. Not my usual, stoic, expressionless stare with tears leaking out, but an outright snotty, whimpering, shuddering, full bodied bawl. It's an epic cry of the sort I've not had since I crushed Jasper's motorcycle. Ethan holds me gently, rubbing my back as I snot all over his shirt.

Increasingly it feels cathartic. I'm no longer crying just for Rachel's tragedy, but I'm crying for all three of us, for sunlit fields, shady oaks, and everything we lost. Lost because of me. Because I was too scared to love, too scared of the vulnerability in apologizing. She would have forgiven without hesitation! But it would have required admitting I loved her too, and this was simply not possible. I chose alone and safe within myself instead. I'm crying for Jasper, his insecurity and pride, not being able to forgive my mother, taking it out on me. I was ten you bastard! I'm crying for not being able to fully give myself to Ethan. To love him in the way he deserves. This notion makes me moan quietly, feeling the most immediately tragic.

Ethan is kneeling in front of me, stroking my head, hushing me sweetly, "It's ok lover. It's ok."

I look up at him, my cheeks red, streaked, puffy. He wipes a few tears away, then makes a show of wiping the snot from my nose with the back of his hand. I smile a little.

"Actually, her letter is the reason I followed you to college. I had no delusion of dating when we graduated high school. We hardly spoke. But I wanted to be there for you whenever you needed me. I wanted to be your friend. I was nervous when I saw you at orientation, but I imagined a nine-year-old Rachel under that tree, her half smile pointed my way, impatiently waving her little hand at me to go ahead. I took a deep breath and walked right up to you. Tried to act like nothing had happened, that we'd been friends the whole time, used being alone in a new place together to my advantage. It worked."

He's right. We picked up right where we left off, back when we were still virgins. From the first day of college, platonically inseparable once again, discarding the platonic part when Samson found his way into my dorm room a few years later.

I hug him close, tight. Looking over his shoulder, I see the picture forgotten on the floor behind him. From this distance it's all Rachel. The full-bodied laugh thrown at the cameraman, that guy John standing there smiling at her. A cliff looms ominously behind them.

Emotionally exhausted, I stand up silently and trudge into the bedroom to lay down. Ethan follows, thinks better of it, walks out. Silence. I'm cried out, and staring at the wall I try to treasure the Rachel I remember. Eventually, I fall asleep.

6

I wake to the dim light of evening, Ethan sitting on the edge of the bed watching me. This feels a bit creepy at first, but then his big goofy grin makes me feel safe.

He gives me an exaggerated wave hello, "Welcome back to your magic cabin, where intrigue awaits around every corner, romance under every sheet!" Slipping his hand under the covers and giving my leg a squeeze.

"You were moaning a little in your sleep, and I was busy reading your thoughts. Couldn't decide if you were having sex or fighting a ghost, but either way I wanted to help!"

Smiling at him lightly, this joke makes me uncomfortable. Ethan's dissertation is something about human connection and gender relations. It's so obviously stemming from our history and relationship I can't bring myself to read it. He tries too hard. I know he just wants to unlock the Susan mystery box, and it comes from loving me deeply, but it does feel he tries to read my mind and has studied psychology for years to learn how. On top of how well we know each other, his effort sometimes invades my private, inner self in a way I cannot allow, leaving me wondering if he's working some psychological Jedi mind trick on me. He doesn't do it maliciously, there's not a malicious bone in Ethan's body, but certainly he gently pries me open. In truth it makes me lock the mystery box even tighter.

I close my eyes again, picturing his classes. Everyone in a circle, séance style, two students in the middle staring at each other. One places his hands on the other's temples, the circle joins hands and hums lightly. Abruptly jerking his hands away, as if burned, 'vegetarian tacos?! Gross.' Everyone laughs. Sheepishly the other student mumbles 'my girlfriend's a vegetarian. I'm hungry.' PhD classes are probably the same, except with impassioned humming, moaning even, and without the shock afterwards. 'Ah, vegetarian tacos. Why do you think the tofu was mayonnaise flavored?' Mumbles of ascent and quiet 'hm, why indeed?'s circulate the room.

He's still watching, head cocked now, wearing Rachel's half smile with an added single eyebrow raised. He knows I've drifted off down some bizarre tangent, a habit of mine.

I poke him on the nose, "You won't guess that one, Ethan the Magnificent."

Frowning lightly at the moniker, he shakes it off and stands, arms out, twirling slowly and offering a regal expression in all directions, "Greetings humble servants," he declares, "the exquisite goddess Susan Marie does not wish her luxurious and succulent depths probed today," winking at me, "the depths of her mind that is!" doing a little skip in place, arms still raised, he nods solemnly, "Two points. Double entendre for the win."

Dropping his arms, looking out the window, "That chipmunk actually came all the way back here while you were sleeping. It was bizarre. Didn't even react when I tried to scare him away. Left on his own, casually, carrying a nut too. Like he owned the place."

I shrug, "Like you said, they must feed him."

Pushing off the bed to get up, searing pain jolts through my right forearm and Ethan steadies me.

Holding my elbow, concerned, he looks me up and down, "How's the head? Memory clearing up?"

I dislodge his grip by sliding into a hug, "That was my forearm actually, it's really bothering me. Banged it on something. No change in the ol' noggin." Touching the back of my head lightly, "Well, do have a mild headache."

He's studying me, brow furrowed, "Maybe the headache and forearm are positives? Evidence Susan's standard grace did in fact cause trauma related amnesia?"

Now adding a small smile, "Actually I can totally see it. You're wearing that crazy sunhat, hiking fast, smacking directly into a low hanging tree branch, and you lash out at the branch to spite it, catching your forearm."

Taking his hand, "Let's go back out to the porch swing. See if we can catch any remaining sunset."

His smile broadens, "I am on board with that! I've got some Advil for your head. I'll grab it. Rendezvous: porch swing!"

Parts of his theory on my amnesia sound vaguely familiar. Not a memory exactly though.

7

Sunlight streaming through the open window, curtains ruffling lightly in a morning breeze. I mentally tally 'Day Two', like I'm some kind of convict, keeping track of the days since my memory jumped ship.

Waking in Ethan's arms is my favorite part of our relationship. In the few moments before fear, or annoyance, sets in, I feel completely safe. Often he gets up to make me coffee before I wake up. A lovely gesture, but I prefer the times I'm awake first, and always savor them.

"I love you," I whisper to him.

Turns out he is awake, sending a mixed message my way with both a squeeze and a frustrated sigh.

Sitting up on an elbow, "We need to talk Susan."

Moment: gone. I eye him wearily, "That sounds ominous. We haven't even been awake five seconds. Coffee."

He nods, "Hold that thought." Momentarily I hear him fumbling around in the kitchen.

Strolling back in with purpose, he sets my coffee on the bedside table. Didn't even make himself a cup. Sitting on the edge of the bed I look up at him, a plea in my eyes not to go down whatever road he has in mind. He's still standing, staring down at me, a sure sign he's on a mission.

"I'm not Jasper."

The room tilts, and I have to brace myself, sending another jolt of pain through my forearm.

Ignoring my startle, he shakes his head, "Actually maybe we don't need to talk. I just need to get this off my chest. I'm sorry I have to, I don't think it's good for us, but 'us' is stagnant." He pauses, "And here we are."

He seems unsure what to do with his hands, looking at them briefly, then sits next to me staring straight ahead. "I am not Jasper. I love you. I always have. No exaggeration, as a point in fact, I have no memory of not loving you. But he locked you up. I thought for years I just needed to find the key and help you unlock. The key's not lost though. You have it. You don't want to use it."

Opening his mouth a few times, he finally gives up on saying anything more. He starts to leave, stopping at the door, hand on the frame and looking halfway back towards me. Not at me. Eyes downcast.

Gently, without malice, "Please don't tell me you love me until you actually do."

Another pause, pregnant this time. Ethan's motionless, statue like, and whispers, "It's ok if you can't, but," he stops, and I have to strain to hear him breathe the rest of the thought, "but I'll need to move on."

Taking his hand from the doorframe, he scratches his neck lightly. Straightens up, blows out a long sigh and nods. Walks out.

Numbly, I sit on the bed until I suddenly realize how badly I need to pee. I've never really considered the possibility of Ethan leaving me.

After the bathroom pit stop, I wander the cabin, and then outside, but he's nowhere to be found. Probably gone for a walk, giving me time to think. It's frighteningly clear this is his last-ditch effort. 'Address Jasper or I'm out.' A card he never wanted to play as he fears it. By now he knows I can't.

Back in the bedroom, I'm breathing too fast, something simmering, trying to find the surface. Seeing the untouched coffee, now cold, makes me suddenly furious and I grab the cup, hurling it through the bedroom door!

Fine! Ruin our goddamn magic cabin journey Ethan! Bad for us is it? You think I can't deal with Jasper do you? There's nothing to deal with!

"That piece of shit is nothing to me!" I scream, slapping the bed as hard as I can.

Everything starts to go black with the pain immediately searing through my forearm! Collapsing on the bed with a whimper, I want to cry with anger, hurt and confusion, but well-honed instinct takes over. The tremble in my lip abruptly stops, leaving a straight, thin line in its wake. Dry eyes, blank, stare at nothing. My face frozen in time, pale. Stone.

I stand and brush off my clothes, straightening them. Realizing I didn't hear the cup smash into anything, I walk over to the bedroom door to survey the damage, but there's none to be found beyond a lengthy streak of coffee heading out the door.

Cocking my head to the side, I finally notice the chipmunk is examining it all the way out in the grass. I guess I threw it straight through the living room, kitchen, and front door, even clearing the porch, not bad. Objectively my rockstar arm, the improbable survival of my Hello Kitty mug, and the potentially caffeinated chipmunk all ought to amuse me, but I feel nothing.

Rolling my neck around as I rub my throbbing forearm gently, I peer about the room. The clutter in the closet grabs my attention, and I shut the door gently. After a moment's thought, I close the bedroom door too, and then the window, drawing the curtain. Sitting on the floor in the dim light, I cross my legs, hands on knees as if to meditate.

"Fuck you Jasper."

8

My daddy had two loves in the garage, a 1978 International Harvester Scout II and a 1941 Indian Four Motorcycle. I later learned the meticulously restored motorcycle would have fetched nearly six figures at a collector's auction, a fact I've no doubt quietly agitated Mom at night, knowing they were sitting on a lottery ticket he wouldn't cash.

No one was allowed near the motorcycle, and he hardly even rode it. I once watched from the garage window as he simply stared at it, drinking a beer, wearing a softly contented expression. I only had eyes for the Scout anyway.

By time I was born, International Harvester built eighteen wheelers, but the Scout II was an early SUV, or maybe a truck, and it was a thing of beauty. Ours once had a soft top, like a jeep, but he removed it and never put it back on. Nothing but metal and vinyl, he carried a trash bag to throw over the radio if we got caught in the rain.

Yes, the Scout ventured from the garage on sunny days, usually with an exuberant little girl bouncing along, wind whipping through her hair, laughing, trying to look casual while willing every stranger to notice, riding shotgun with her daddy. Topping it off, the Scout was a pale baby blue, just like my eyes! I loved everything about it.

Not the type to be windblown and disheveled, Alice didn't like the Scout, but I believed he chose me. It was our thing. He often ran errands in it, and I'd charge into the garage whenever I heard that particular jingle of the tiny skull and crossbones on the key ring, planting myself in my seat before he even opened the driver's door. The moment he cranked on that massive engine, gently gyrating my little body around, I'd open my mouth wide and hum loudly just to hear my voice waver with the engine's rumble, smiling up at him. He'd chuckle at my excitement and grind it into gear.

Just before heading out, he'd ensure my seatbelt was extra tight. He never could fix the passenger door's catch, and it would sometimes open with a turn, swinging wildly. I'd nearly tumble out, squealing happily, grabbing for the door, unable to reach, then he would jerk the wheel sharply on the next curve, yelling 'Arms! Legs!' and I'd throw myself out of the way towards him. The door would slam, bouncing against the truck's frame, and I'd lunge back the other way, latching on to it, trying to hold it shut, ecstatic with my part in this drama. He'd smile the whole time, proud of his little girl's lack of fear. It was the most affection I ever got from him.

Most days he'd take me to Joey's after whatever errand, and I'd sit on the warm hood while he casually leaned next to me, silently eating ice cream cones together. He'd often chat with the teenage boys, and plenty of grown men too, about the truck's particulars, usually cranking up the engine for everyone to admire. I always felt so important, so cool, included in this ritual.

On that fateful day, when a bored ten-year-old made a simple mistake, we hadn't taken the Scout out recently; I wanted to feel the engine's rumble! I'd seen him do it hundreds of times. I knew to press the clutch, turn the key, no big deal. I had to kind of crouch in front of the seat to get the clutch all the way to the floor, and that glorious growling engine was even more magnificent down there! Plus I made it happen! Little me! I was busy having fantasies about starting the Scout for him and then sitting in his lap instead of the passenger seat when I noticed it was rolling forward. In a panic I popped the clutch and slammed both feet on the brake!

It was in first gear of course, and that massive engine tried to catch! Already rolling, it powerfully lurched into the garage wall with a sickening crunch before stalling. The 1941 Indian Four, my daddy's pride and joy, well, it was parked between the Scout and the wall. The concrete, cinder block wall.

The Scout's solid metal bumper showed no mercy, more than a decade of careful restoration demolished. In shock I released the brake and the Scout rolled back a little, allowing the crushed motorcycle to topple over in a heap. A few pieces of metal rolled quietly away, and something rattled gently for a moment longer. The final whimpers of a murder.

Mom rushed in at the noise, stopping short at the door, hand to her mouth. For the briefest moment I saw the flash of a smile, quickly replaced by horror. "Suzy, what have you done?"

I spent the next few hours blubbering, vomiting twice. Mom held me for a while, but she was shaking slightly, her agitation and fear making me cry harder. I asked her to leave me alone.

I was in my room cowering in the corner when I heard him come home. The fight was spectacular, a monumental roar rolling through my closed door, and I flinched continually as if punched by the harsh staccato. I heard several crashes I later discovered were both living room lamps and the bowl from the coffee table.

At first it was all my father, a furious, insensible berating of my mother, the family, and me, me, me! Everything I had ever done wrong pierced and cut me through the door! Covering my ears, squinching my eyes closed tightly, failing to block it out, I rocked and cried, trembling in fear and shame.

The fight devolved into anything that was frustrating him, or had in the last decade. My mother took it, letting him blow off the steam.

Eventually, two lamps, a bowl, and one motorcycle poorer, it grew quiet. I could hear them talking, but not the conversation. After a few minutes, it became heated again, but this time with mom screaming too. She bellowed 'You can't tell her!' with such fury I felt a feverish chill. Then the vile, lightning crack of flesh on flesh!

Silence. My mother is unconscious.

⊷⊶

Now my breath catches. Sitting on the cabin floor, I'm truly reliving this memory. I am in this space, Ethan, for you. This is a cruel, torturous journey of your devising. Briefly I entertain the notion that our entire relationship is actually a cold psychological exercise to cure me. I am his dissertation, his masterpiece, carefully orchestrated for this moment. I try to relax, breathe deep. I dive in.

⊷⊶

Daddy opens the door. I expect him to be smoldering, a veritable picture of pure rage. He's not. He's calm. He leans against my door frame.

"You're not mine."

I stare up at him from across the room, not understanding. He doesn't elaborate, so after a long moment I stammer a, "Wh-What?"

"You're not mine." Looking at his fingernails, "Your mother got knocked up while I was deployed. Some two-bit piece of shit took advantage of her loneliness and the stress of raising Alice alone. I didn't want you, but she convinced me."

He stares at me. I have his meaning now, but not his intent. A hole begins to grow in the pit of my stomach.

Gesturing towards the living room, "Your mother's a convincing woman. I can't believe I hit her. That's your fault too."

I lean cautiously to my left, peering around daddy's legs and seeing mom's feet, motionless amongst the detritus of the broken bowl.

He shifts his stance, blocking my view of the living room, shrugs at me, "You don't belong under my roof. I want to kick you out, boarding school at least, but she won't have it."

Glancing back towards his unconscious wife, his face melds into an expression awash with guilt and shame, "Now I've gone too far. I'm not going to fight with her about it. Once she wakes up, I'll start the years of apologizing for my temper,"

Turning back to me, all expression draining away, "Which you made me lose."

He sighs, looking down and shaking his head, "She's a good woman. It'd be a fitting grand hurrah for you if I lose her. You, the walking reminder of when I wasn't there for her, of when she strayed."

He's quiet for a moment, processing. I'm certain his precious motorcycle flickers through his mind, as his eyes harden and he suddenly takes an aggressive step into my room, jabbing a finger towards me, inadvertently flinging a speck of blood onto the wall. I cower, sniveling, making myself as small as possible in the corner, the crack of flesh on flesh still reverberating through my brain. I am blind with the terror of my own beating I am sure has arrived!

My abject fear deflates him a little, and he drops his hand, but the malice remains in his tone, "If you ever do anything like this again, ever touch any of my things, ever put one more toe in my way, that is it! She will not be able to save you, not even boarding school! The street."

He hesitates, then to himself, "No, that will be the compromise. I'll push for the street and she'll accept boarding school."

Smiling a little, he locks eyes with me, "Boarding school. The cheapest, most dangerous one I can find."

Glancing down at his palms, he turns the right over, examining his knuckles, reddened, two of them bleeding, a rivulet of blood tracking down his middle finger to the tip. He smears the blood with his other hand, keeping it from dripping onto my floor. Shakes his head.

Looking back up at me, his face flat, "Now you know."

I stare, my mouth agape, a hiccup of a whimper escaping. Suddenly parts of my life develop a sharper focus. I always felt Alice was his favorite, he treated her so differently. The side-eyed looks he always gave mom when I disappointed them. Occasional unexplained glares directed my way. An entire lifetime of semi-indifference takes new meaning! The hole in my stomach grows.

Beginning to weep quietly again, "D-daddy?"

He puffs out some air, exasperated, "I just explained it to you, bitch, I'm not your daddy."

A beat passes, he looks around the room as if just noticing it, "My name is Jasper."

At this he shakes his head at me. Turns around. Walks out.

I cannot process this. The hole expands, a black ooze swallows me and desperately I reach for the safety of fantasy, escaping from a reality I do not understand. Fighting nausea, desolation, and a suffocating emptiness, I close my eyes.

I am in our field, I see the oak. Rachel pushes Ethan playfully, he throws himself to the ground with a dramatic flourish. They're laughing and wave me over. I hesitate, closing my mouth, which was still agape. Love can hurt. Love can tear a hole in your stomach, your heart, maybe your soul.

I swallow hard and turn away, to a castle. Walking in I pull up the drawbridge, lock the door, lower the gates. I sit in an ornate leather chair facing the door and pat the shotgun at my side. Feeling calm, I walk to the stone fireplace, large enough to lay down in, toss in the key, watch it melt.

Opening my eyes, I'm back in my bedroom. My face is stone. Salty streaks of wasted tears paint my cheeks, a warrior's pattern highlighting the thin line of my mouth.

Emotionless, staring blankly, calmly I offer the room, "I'm sorry I crushed your motorcycle Jasper."

Getting up, I crawl into bed and stretch, sigh. At peace, I head into a dreamless sleep.

Fleetingly, I wonder if my mother woke up.

9

Stretching my legs out on the floor, I feel that same cold, steely resolve I've nourished for so many years. Safe within myself, no one can hurt me that way again. I smile lightly, thinking Ethan is right, there actually was a key. I'd forgotten that little castle fantasy.

I shake my arms out, roll my neck around again and run my hands through my hair, fingernails massaging my scalp. Jostle that emotional ice a bit, knock some off. Rubbing my shoulders, I sigh and close my eyes once more, picturing the castle.

❧❧

Young Rachel and Ethan are under the oak, waving me over, and a sharp lump in my throat accompanies Rachel's laugh. I hold up a finger towards them, as if to say, 'Hang on, I'll be right over.' I head to the castle, the drawbridge, gate, and door creaking open at my approach.

It's cold and empty. I suppose my imagination didn't see fit to manifest the ten-year-old version of me. Everything is in disuse, cobwebs abound.

I stride over to the massive fireplace, noting a splash of melted iron amongst the ash. First brushing the iron stain lightly with my fingertips, I then settle onto the cold stone floor for a moment, taking it in.

Certainly this was a turning point in my life. I wonder briefly how different things would be if I had never started the Scout that day. It doesn't matter though.

Tossing some leafy detritus into the fireplace, I don't feel any connection to the castle. I feel silly coming here to admire a spot of melted metal. A childhood fantasy, a purpose served, emotionally ingrained, then abandoned.

◈◈

Back in reality, I stand up quickly. Ethan is right, I do hold the key. I don't think it has anything to do with Jasper though, despite being the catalyst. The catharsis I experienced earlier, crying over Rachel's letter, that's the key.

Walking back into the living room, I find the picture still laying on the floor near the couch. Gently I pick it up, holding it lightly with both hands. Almost Rachel throws her full-bodied laugh at me.

"Rachel, I'm sorry." I take a deep breath. "I'm sorry I couldn't love you the way you loved me. I miss you." Eyes wet now, softer, "I'm sorry I wasn't there when you needed me."

I carefully place the picture back on the bookshelf, staring at her for a moment. I'm not certain I just magically unlocked my heart, or will feel any differently towards Ethan, but I do feel better.

I smile a bit ruefully, wondering if I just played out Ethan's strategy as planned, if he hoped to direct me here all along. Feeling safe in this moment, the idea of him being so entrenched in my head is no longer threatening. Ethan the Magnificent. I hope he'll be able to see his clients the way he sees me, will make him an astounding therapist.

I shake my head, wanting to talk to him about it, share my journey and tiny insights. Where is he anyway?

It's his habit to take long walks. I think he forces himself to do it, knowing I need space. What I really need is a run. Early afternoon. I've got plenty of time to throw down a ten miler or so, clear the head.

Back on the main trail, though it feels like the first time to my addled brain, I admire the Deus Ex Machina sign and nearly hidden trail to the cabin. It is bizarre, and magnificent all the same.

I take a few minutes to thoroughly mark the cabin trail with two big branches and a pile of sticks, a downright trip hazard. I don't know which direction we hiked in from, but guessing we were facing the sign and Ethan would take new trail past it, I start my Garmin and jog in the opposite direction.

There's nothing but smooth, easy trail, lined by trees, and I cruise. After almost five miles the forest falls away as I come around a corner, revealing a rocky outcropping next to a cliff.

I cheer at the change in scenery, doing a little skip. Following the tree line around the bend, I see the trail continues along the cliff. The sort that always make me nervous to run, but feeling confident on my feet today I plow on through, noticing it's where Rachel's doppelganger stood in the picture.

I take in the view as I jog. It is truly lovely! Rolling hills, green with nothing but trees. Distant, larger mountains, but not the Rockies. Oregon, I think, maybe Washington.

Lost in the view, not watching my feet too closely, I nearly step on a chipmunk huddled in the middle of the trail. Too late to stop, I plant my front foot in order to hop right over him, but he suddenly stands straight up on his feet, throwing his paws in the air, chittering at me like a madman!

Startled, brain sending simultaneous stop and go signals, my planted foot falters and I fail to jump at all, sliding forward, losing my balance, toppling right on top of him.

He scurries out of the way as my momentum carries me onto my hands, then shoulder as I instinctively fling myself away from the cliff!

The trail curves though.

I spread eagle as I slide off the trail into the scree of the cliff, burying the side of my face and head in it for more traction when I fail to slow in the loose rock. My right forearm strikes something stationary, a lightning bolt of pain, then numbness below the elbow. The jolt slows me, and I imagine grabbing with my invisible forearm, sending every signal I can to those muscles. My legs begin to swing past my upper body, and I'm able to grab the stationary rock I smashed into with my other hand! In a final surge of functionality for my right arm I brace with it while pulling with the left. I hook my left elbow around the rock! I stop.

Panting, heart pounding in my ears, I register everything below my ribcage is hanging into free air! I kick my legs gently, trying to find purchase without moving too much. Nothing. My right arm is not working, I feel incredibly weak with pain and the shock of what just happened. I desperately grasp the stationary rock.

Looking up the slope, I see the chipmunk, still standing on his hind legs. Dimly I register he looks like a miniature grizzly bear, standing tall with his arms up like that. But now he's holding a nut, his head cocked.

He throws it down the slope. Lightly it bounces my way.

I can't pull myself up with one arm. I can't find anything with my feet. I have never felt so trapped, helpless.

Suddenly I am choking on something, and worse, all the air is being sucked from my lungs. I gag violently.

I fall.

PART III

*One day Alice came to a fork in the road
and saw a Cheshire cat in a tree.
'Which road do I take?' she asked.
'Where do you want to go?' was his response.
'I don't know,' Alice answered.
'Then,' said the cat, 'it doesn't matter.'*

Alice in Wonderland, Lewis Carroll

1

Breathe.

I glance about to find myself in a rickety cabin I explored as a child. Awash with memory, I can feel the magic and mystery invoked by that bright-eyed little girl. It was all around as I tentatively tiptoed, a treasure waiting in every closet, behind every book, under a secret floorboard. Today I stand stock still, an emotional chill leaving goosebumps in its wake. Instantly familiar, yet out of place in time, the warm sunlight sparkling on the dust I've stirred. I inhale the stale, amber atmosphere. My breath catches. For a moment the walls act strangely, arching towards the depth of my morning yawn. No. Making the sound of a dying seagull, "bhrugurhubrhu!" I shake the sleep away. Is that the sound a dying seagull makes? I've never been here. Where the hell am I even? Surreal. Where's the F-ing coffee?

Heading into the kitchen, I find a small Tupperware of coffee, my pour over filter and Hello Kitty mug all laid out on the counter, ready for the morning I suppose. Fumbling with the propane stove, I get a pot of water going. I lean on the counter, feeling confused.

I have my eyes closed, listening for the water to boil, when Rachel wraps her arms around my waist from behind, kissing me lightly on the earlobe, whispering, "Good morning gorgeous."

Turning around I take her into my arms as she pecks me on the lips, but my sense of disorientation expands rapidly, the comfort of the last few months dating clashing with something else, something ill-defined and out of reach. Her presence is simultaneously perfectly natural and completely implausible!

Trying to focus on the clock behind her, the hands appear to jump and the room tilts impossibly. Looking a little frightened, Rachel tries to hold me up as I stumble, blindly throwing my arm out for the wall. Sharp, lightning pain shoots through my forearm! With a yelp I pull my arm back and we collapse in a heap on the floor.

Letting out a sputter of laughter, she disentangles herself from me, "What the hell was that Suzy? Are you ok?"

Looking up at her, I'm unable to focus completely, and she doesn't look quite right. Almost Rachel, but not quite, a doppelganger of some kind. Blinking a few times rapidly, she comes into focus, the half smile currently sporting a puzzled flavor. The smile slides away as she notes the confusion and fear in my eyes.

Scooting back away from her, the room stabilizes. Rachel, my lifelong friend and recent lover, on her knees in front of me wearing an expression of confused concern. I feel an all-consuming sense of relief to see her there, watching me worriedly. Inexplicably, I am also overwhelmed with a profound sense of loss I cannot define!

Choking on a sob, I reach out for her plaintively, and she pulls me into her lap, wrapping me up right there on the floor.

I begin to cry. Not my usual, stoic, expressionless stare with tears leaking out, but an outright snotty, whimpering, shuddering, full bodied bawl. It's an epic cry of the sort I've not had since I crushed Jasper's motorcycle. She holds me gently, stroking my hair as I snot all over her shirt.

Increasingly it feels cathartic, but I don't know why. Fleetingly I think of sunlit fields, shady oaks, and wind in the leaves. I sigh and take her hand.

2

We sit there in silence for a long time. Rachel's able to reach the stove from the floor, and we share coffee out of my Hello Kitty mug, leaning side by side against the cabinets.

I'm cried out, feeling calm. I know she is waiting for some explanation, and I wish I had one. Through the screen door we watch a chipmunk scurrying around on the deck. A robin lights on the railing.

Finally I blow out a long breath, deflating like a balloon, feeling a little embarrassed, "I don't know what to say."

She eyes me over the mug, "What were you thinking when it started?"

I close my eyes, trying to capture the chaos bouncing through my brain when she first hugged me, "Nothing exactly, it was violently confusing." I shrug, "I've never felt so overpoweringly disoriented."

Processing a moment longer, I offer, "Something about you. When I looked at you, I felt absolutely despondent and incredibly relieved in opposite and equal amounts, at the exact same time." Thinking about it, my eyes try to water again, "I still feel it a little. It's bizarre."

Still staring intently, she says. "Deus Ex Machina."

This comment is so incongruous I sit up straighter, turning towards her, "What do you mean?"

Furrowing her brow, "The sign at the trailhead. The whole reason you wanted to take this trail? I just meant this whole place is bizarre."

I debate about telling her I don't remember how we got here, but decide this morning has been weird enough. I need to sort things out before worrying her any more.

Taking a sip, she tilts her head lightly towards me, "You said that means 'God from the Machine'? I don't get it."

Glad to move into something I understand, "It's a literary term. Comes from Greek tragedies, when the hero faces impossible odds and has hit rock bottom. There is no way for him to win, so to speak, and the solution is the appearance of a god wielding the power to rescue him." I relax back against the cabinets, continuing, "In the actual play, the actor portraying the god would be lowered from above the stage with a crane of some sort, a machine. Hence 'God from the Machine.'"

Pausing, I gauge her interest before elaborating, "Today it represents a seemingly random plot device used to solve an unsolvable problem."

She nods, "The good guy is out of bullets, desperate, the bad guy holding a gun on him, laughing maniacally. Suddenly a piano falls on the bad guy. Whack!"

Smiling, "Crude, but yeah. Looney Tunes definitely favored the Deus Ex Machina approach. In modern literature you hope for something a little more subtle, maybe meaningful."

Rachels stretches, getting up she runs her hand along the doorframe, "So this cabin is our God from the Machine huh?

What's our unsolvable problem?" She smiles mischievously at me, like we're involved in some mystery.

Standing up too, I sigh, wrapping my arms around her shoulders from behind while she rests a hand on my wrist, looking outside together, taking it in quietly. It does feel like I'm in a mystery of some kind. I don't remember how I got here. I'm awash with bizarre and confusing emotions. What is this? I must have hit my head and really shook something loose!

Patting my arm, she pulls out of my hug, "There's a double porch swing. I'll make another cup of coffee and join you."

Rachel sits down next to me and nuzzles into my side, flinging her legs across my lap. We take in the trees and the breeze, the robin's feathers ruffling, still sitting on the railing. It doesn't seem to care, beak nestled into its wing, looking asleep. The chipmunk scurries over and sits on its haunches in front of us, staring, head cocked to the side.

I stop the swing with my toes, not wanting to scare him, "The locals are pretty friendly." He's holding a nut, and actually throws it, then claws his way up the banister and sits right next to the robin on the railing. Rachel laughs, infectious as always, and I have to chuckle too.

She reaches down, picking up the nut, "I've never seen a chipmunk throw something. Talented!" Turning his way, "Got your breakfast little buddy!" holding it towards him.

He just stares. The robin wakes and scoots a few inches from the chipmunk, takes in Rachel, then me, nestles back into her wing.

I start rocking again. The vibe is so peaceful, the weight of the morning lifts and I give her a squeeze. At the moment I'm too content to really care how I got here, or what the emotional rollercoaster was about.

She looks up at me, a rare full smile instead of the half. I can tell she's relieved to feel me relax. Poking me on the nose, she laughs lightly, "I love this place. Did you see the sign above the door?"

We both look over. Rachel leaning backwards, with me holding her legs to provide leverage.

> *You Are Here*
> *All Who Seek*
> *All Who Wander*
> *-- And Wonder --*
> *You Are Welcome*

I laugh, the day's confusion morphing into a kind of giddiness, "That. Is. Spectacular! I absolutely want it for our place. Can you take a picture?"

Grabbing my hand, she nibbles my fingers gently, bouncing her eyebrows up and down, "I love it when you talk about *our* place." Frowning slightly against my fingers, "Both our phones are dead though. I had mine on airplane even." She shrugs, "Guess there's value to having a real camera instead of the ol' cell phone."

Disappointed, I put a finger to my temple, winking slowly, "Click, click, click. Got it!"

Rachel still has the nut, tossing it back and forth like a hot potato. The swing creaks. The chipmunk stares. Patting her hand to stop the nervous tossing, I gesture at the chipmunk, "He's creeping me out, I think he wants his breakfast back."

She looks down at the nut, sitting up suddenly, "What the flying fuck?" Hands it to me, wearing a bemused look.

Taking it, I immediately see what startled her. Someone scratched 'Fentanyl' in tiny letters across its surface.

I stop the swing, sitting up straighter as well. We exchange identical looks, amused, wide eyed, eyebrows raised. I carefully place the nut on the railing next to the chipmunk, like it's dangerous or something, shaking my finger at him, 'Tsk, tsk.'

He looks at it but doesn't move. The robin wakes again, seeming to side-eye him.

Rachel grabs a pillow to put against the armrest so she can lean back and look at me more directly. I start rocking again. Together we lower our eyebrows and smile.

Leaning back, stretching my arm out on the top of the swing, "What's Fentanyl? Isn't it that party drug?"

Rachel shrugs, "I heard it's part of the opioid epidemic. A hundred times stronger than morphine or something. Some party."

Shaking my head, "We'll have to keep an eye on this here chipmunk," winking at him, "Not as sweet as he looks!"

She's staring off into the trees, "Why would someone carve that into a nut?" pausing a beat, "I'll bet some addict was here. Therapy. Scratch your addition into a nut, throw it into the trees. Symbolic."

I nod, giving her an appreciative smile, "That's totally it. I like it. What should we scratch into our nuts?"

Rachel bursts out laughing, and I quickly join. Through staccato giggles, she stammers, "I know plenty of guys, who should carve, their nuts, and throw them into the trees!"

Leaning forward, she slides a hand between my legs, "If you had nuts I'd carve 'Dick' into them and chuck 'em as far as possible. Get it out of your system!"

This makes me a little uncomfortable, but she doesn't mean it maliciously, and it's impossible not to laugh with Rachel. I take her hand in mine though, placing it safely on my thigh. She kisses me on the neck, still chuckling, nuzzling into my side again.

The chipmunk kicks the nut off the railing.

3

Resting my chin in my hands while peeing, I take a moment to admire the nicely appointed bathroom, kneading my toes into the opulent rug, taking in the dingy skylight.

Suddenly Rachel's yell, "Suzy!" stops me mid-stream. She sounds more angry than scared, and for a second I try to restart to finish the performance, but a more fearful, "Seriously, get the fuck in here!" makes me give up and hustle into the living room.

She's standing stock still, staring at the bookshelf. Seeing me she points emphatically, "Alfred has a fucking picture of me!"

I follow her finger and sure enough, there's a framed photo of Rachel on top of the bookshelf. She's standing on the edge of a cliff, throwing a full-bodied laugh at the cameraman. Ethan and some other guy are next to her, laughing hard as well.

"Who's Alfred?"

She waves this off, "Just what I've named the cabin owner. Why the fuck is there a picture of me here?" Looking around the room and over her shoulder, she rubs both arms in a self-hug, "I am so creeped out right now."

I can't explain its presence, but somehow the picture doesn't feel out of place to me. I pull Rachel's head against my shoulder and pick up the photo so we can both see. The other guy is taller and has his arm around Ethan's neck, pretending to punch him in the stomach.

"Who's he? I kinda want to chew on his legs a little."

She side-eyes me for a moment, annoyed by this reaction, "That's John, Ethan's best friend. He does have nice legs." A little exacerbated, she pushes away from my shoulder, crossly stamping her foot, "Why doesn't this freak you out?"

I shrug, "It is weird I guess." Thinking a moment I offer, "Alfred must have known we were coming."

She throws her hands in the air, "Right! I didn't even think about that! Not only does he have a picture of me, but he knew we were coming and prominently displayed it on his bookshelf. This is right out of some Stephen King novel. A creepy hint that we've been watched and expected. Any moment a ghost or deranged axe murdered is going to pop out, eat our souls or chop us to bits. Probably both."

I peer at her, feeling a twinge of jealousy at how much time she must spend with Ethan, as clearly his imagination is pouring out of her right now. Shaking it off, I smile at her, "I'm sure there's a logical explanation. Maybe we were set up to come here. Seems reasonable that Deus Ex Machina is directed at me."

This calms her a little, and I see her face soften as something dawns on her.

Now her half smile creeps up, "Those complete and total dorks. That's one hundred percent something Ethan and John would do. I told them I was planning this trip!" Letting out a big sigh, "Wow, they freaked me out! I owe them both a good hard smack."

Breaking into a full smile now, she looks around again, this time excitedly, "I wonder if they're here somewhere!"

Leaving me abruptly she runs outside, "Hey you douchebags! The jig is up! Come on in! Did you bring beer?"

I follow her outside, picture in hand. We're greeted only by silence. The chipmunk and robin sit next to each other on the railing, staring.

"Now that's creepy." I say, gesturing at the pair.

Rachel makes a little aggressive lunge at them, but they don't react. She half shrugs, a purely Rachel gesture, "They're just used to being fed."

Turning her attention back to the woods, scanning the tree line for movement, "If they come in to scare us in the middle of the night I am going to be seriously hacked off."

Cupping her hands around her mouth she yells, "Come out now or you will fall fully into perv territory! I'll have her naked, sweaty legs wrapped around my face later!" Jabbing her thumb in my general direction.

Rachel's assertation amuses me a little, and inspires a little rush between my legs. Noting this I actually feel relieved, marveling at how what was largely a need for emotional intimacy is blossoming into a semi-normal sexual response. Pavlovian. Maybe I really can be a lesbian, which would lighten a guilt I've been carrying since she first took me to bed. I've definitely been using her sexual desire to satisfy my emotional one, and have felt since the beginning we were doomed as a couple. She turns me on, sorta, but it's not the same.

Suddenly I notice she's watching me silently, head cocked to the side. Ethan used to do that too, whenever I was staring off, mentally chasing some tangent. Gazing back at her, fleetingly I wonder if the way they understood me created the depth of our childhood friendship, or maybe inspired why I pushed them away. Actually I'm certain it's both. There's a lesson in there somewhere! Suzy, no more pushing people away simply because they know who you truly are.

I take a deep breath, closing my eyes, Suzy, it's ok to be vulnerable. Opening them again, I see she's still watching. I laugh lightly and can't help but smile at her.

Content to see a positive outcome from my mental departure, she elects not to ask. Gesturing at the picture, forgotten in my hand, she sighs, "They're not here. No chance that wouldn't have pulled them out of the woods. We'd have heard man giggles before we even saw them! Too bad though."

Smiling mischievously, she takes the picture from me, "Bet it means there's more surprises for us here though! No way they trekked up here just to leave a picture."

Looking intently at it now, "I don't remember this. Few years ago at least. Early grad school maybe."

She scratches the back of her neck and looks around again, uneasy. I can tell she's wondering if her theory is right after all. But it must be. What other explanation is there?

The chipmunk and robin haven't moved, still on the railing and absolutely staring at us. I bend down to their eye level, "Do you know this Alfred fellow? Is he a trustworthy sort?"

Keeping eye contact with the chipmunk, gently I place my hand on the railing, slowly, slowly. Right, next, to, them. The chipmunk looks at my hand, bends, sniffs my thumb, looks back. Rising from his haunches, he stands up tall, gradually raising his arms too. I nudge Rachel, who's watching intently too. He looks like a miniature grizzly bear.

We stand this way in silence, the moment pregnant. No one moves, except the little grizzly who opens and closes his mouth a few times, like he has something to say. Somehow it feels familiar, despite the chipmunk's bizarre behavior. He could be worshipping me, or perhaps casting a spell.

Eventually he lowers his arms, though still holding eye contact. The robin looks at him, back at me, takes off. Startled, the chipmunk looks after her, looks back at me for a beat, then scurries down the railing and off into the trees.

I lean against the railing, intensely amused, and glance back at Rachel. Her mouth is open, but seeing my expression she laughs, "Probably went looking for his Fentanyl nut."

Shaking my head I'm snickering too, "Ah, the plight of the addict!"

4

Rachel sits on the porch swing, guiding me over next to her and placing the photo on the railing facing us. She puts her feet on either side of it and rocks us gently with her toes.

Looking at the guy John in the picture again, a thought occurs to me, "I thought you were Ethan's best friend?"

Rachel blushes. "Ah, well we're all best friends I guess. John sorta replaced you to be honest."

This takes me aback. I had no idea Rachel and Ethan were running around as a threesome again, with some random dude filling my role! I try to picture muscles here doing a little ballerina, hula dance to make them laugh. This makes me chuckle, but I shake it off. His arm around Ethan and all their expressions are clearly genuine. I am awash with jealousy!

"He's a really good guy actually. You'd like him. He's even a writer." She notes my guarded interest and continues, "His first book was a lot like yours in fact. In the sense that it was an emotional exploration with Ethan and I both as character inspirations. It was almost like he picked up where you left off, yours about our childhood and his starting in undergrad. Yours: loss of innocence, coming of age, and his: putting life back together, connection as adults." She smiles, whispering conspiratorially, "I liked yours better though."

I nod slightly, acknowledging the compliment, but my mind is racing. This news is flabbergasting. I was replaced by a writer who is emotionally bonded with my childhood best friends, and deeply enough to use them as source material! Unreal.

Suddenly it occurs to me to wonder if I would recognize them in the book. "Would I have read it?"

She shakes her head, "Doubt it. He hasn't had the commercial success you have." She side-eyes me, pausing a moment, "It's called *A Butterfly Split the Oak*."

I sit straight up in the swing, abruptly turning to face her, "Did he steal the title from our old oak tree?!"

She chuckles, "Well, let's be fair here. That tree is part of Ethan and I too, and we're featured in the story. Bonding as adults, well, I think it's natural to talk about your childhoods and how it got you where you are today. His was seriously messed up, and he was always fascinated by the idea of best friends escaping to a secret hideaway. He knows all kinds of stories about the three of us."

This mollifies me a bit, imagining my replacement had to do loads of research on me and my friends to slip into place.

Sitting back in the swing, curious, I ask, "Am I in it?"

She jabs me in the ribs, "Probably would be if you hadn't dropped off the face of the earth. He wrote the Ethan and Rachel characters as a twosome, saying he couldn't use you for inspiration without permission." She shrugs, "Most of it takes place in our twenties anyway. That old oak only appears a few times in flashback scenes."

Reaching over to muss my hair, "You're taking this way too seriously. It's actually freaking spectacular! I've been debating how to suggest it now that I'm bringing you back into the fold. We absolutely need to be a foursome! You and Ethan bury the hatchet." I frown, but she waves this off aggressively, "No. It's already buried, just acknowledge it together and move on. Period. It will be like old times, except you and John will be best friends too. It's so perfect it makes me giddy!"

Her face softens, voice taking a more serious tone, and she takes both my hands in hers. "I mean it Suzy, the idea fills me with happiness. Even before you and I started dating I would imagine it in bed at night when I was feeling down. I'd think of our laughter, you doing some silly dance, spinning, Ethan's goofy smile while John manhandled him, me tickling John to make him let go, then you tackling all three of us into a friendship fleshpile. I'd hold the thought to my chest until I was full."

She picks up the picture and shakes it in my face, "Actually this is brilliant. We could easily be watching you!"

Her description and intensity take my breath away. I've had similar fantasies over the years, always as children though, and minus this John character of course. Is it possible?

She gently props the picture up with us in the swing, emphasizing the idea that we're all together, admires it for a moment. Then she takes my hands again, a little plea in her eyes.

Looking down at her hands in mine, hope clashing with reality makes my eyes water. "I dunno Rach. I was absolutely hateful to Ethan."

She lets go of my hands with a huff. After a moment she smacks me on the shoulder hard enough to sting. "Get over yourself Suzy. He forgave you a long time ago. We all know you just can't accept the vulnerability of apologizing." This stings too.

Morose, I look up into her eyes, knowing she's right but still unable to stomach the idea of forgiving myself enough to apologize. It's like I'm punishing myself by withholding Ethan's friendship.

"You're right about my vulnerability, but it's so much deeper! I," taking a breath I lean back, staring straight up at the roof, a tear tracking down my cheek, "I couldn't stand his forgiveness. I don't deserve it. Did he tell you what I did?"

She reaches up, wiping the tear away with her thumb, "No. He was pretty tight lipped about the details in fact. Nothing could be so terrible as to warrant separating the three of us for what? Twelve, thirteen years? Is that when you had your falling out?" She pauses a beat, pokes me in the side. "Nothing."

Quietly I murmur, "Fourteen years. We were fifteen."

We swing for a moment, the air heavy. "We were drunk Rachel. Fuck." I squinch my eyes tightly, preparing to barrel ahead and spit it out for the first time. I whisper, "I suggested he raped me."

At first I feel a little release with the confession, and let out a deep breath, deflating like a balloon. Then shame rolls in, making me nauseous, and I swallow hard three or four times, trying not to reproduce the PB&J she made me for lunch. Finally I look over at Rachel, who is staring wide eyed, one hand covering her mouth.

Lowering her hand she murmurs, "Are we talking about the same Ethan? The sweetest boy I have ever known? No, that's not even right. The sweetest person. He's got the heart of a special ed kindergarten teacher melded with the demeanor of a puppy."

Somehow this comment brings my cat, Samson, to mind, incongruous. Samson is a sweet kitty, but I've never associated him with puppies or Ethan. Or kindergarten teachers for that matter. I shake it off, ignoring her rhetorical question, and lean my head into my hands, letting my fingers slide into my hair. I sigh.

I give my entire body a little shake, blow out another deflating breath, slip into full on confession mode. "Of course it was nothing like that. It was incredibly sweet, loving. He kept asking if it was ok despite my mounting encouragement and excitement. He held my cheek, or my hand, almost too tentative and awkward to touch my breasts. Lots of eye contact and gentle kisses. Shit Rachel, I have friends who've still never been loved that way!" I exclaim. "Ethan managed it for our mutual loss of virginity. Magical really."

Looking past her, remembering, "He held me after, shaking slightly. I was suddenly stiff with fear, fingertips laying on his arm across my chest, staring blankly up at the leaves, watching the shifting light, my other hand tightly gripping a root by my hip and holding on for dear life. I was able to relax when I realized he was asleep, and I carefully pried his arm off me, snuck off. Left him there under that oak."

I lean back in the swing, again finding comfort in unloading the burden. "Avoided him all week in school, and you gave me his note, begging to meet at the oak on Saturday. That's when I did it. I don't know how I rationalized it."

Turning towards her, I take Rachel's hands again, searching her face for the forgiveness I do not deserve. "Please. Oh god. I was terrified! Fifteen years old and I loved him! But not in the way he loved me. I didn't understand it. I still don't! And he touched me in a place I could not allow. Something deep, yes, somewhere so vulnerable! Behind a locked door I thought was safe. I had to slam it shut. I had to! Lest everything spill out. Rachel I spent that week falling apart!"

I pause, closing my eyes, trying to regain control, "Somehow it was the only way to feel safe again."

Letting go of her hands I rub my neck. "I was truly hateful. I said he raped me, and if he didn't leave me alone I'd call the cops. That maybe I'd call the cops anyway, to protect you and the other girls at school. Fuck me. Fuck me! I hated myself for it but couldn't stop! I made every effort to leave him waiting for that loud knock on his door, cops and handcuffs outside. He tried to soothe me, tears streaming down his face, but that just scared me all the more, made me angrier!"

Picking a sliver of wood off the swing, I flick it over the railing, gazing at the trees blankly. "He actually started bawling, apologizing like a madman, completely losing control. A part of me was dying to take it all back, enfold him into my arms and beg for forgiveness right then, comfort him. But I couldn't. I just couldn't! I turned and left him there. He didn't follow. We've hardly spoken since."

I look over at Rachel again right as she slaps me. Hard, knocking me into the arm of the swing. I steady myself with a hand on the ground, the other gently touching my cheek, aflame. I look at her, my eyes wild, afraid.

She rubs the palm of her hand on her shirt, no doubt on fire as well. Remarkably, her eyes become kind, and the half smile drifts into place.

Nodding once, she pokes me in the side again, "Ok. That's done. You deserved that. I hope it bruises."

I had frozen in place, with my hand still on the ground, and I ease myself back into the swing. "Well I don't think you got my eye, which surely would have blossomed into an impressive shiner." I rub my cheek a little, "Maybe though. That had some serious force."

Looking out at the trees now, she nods again slowly. "Well, I've had too much practice with men at bars. Somehow a lipstick lesbian such as myself always attracts the worst sorts, like I'm actually straight, hitting on women because I'm loose and desperate for their attention, or hoping for a threesome, either way a chauvinistic pig's dream girl. And they're so goddamn aggressive and handsy! You've really got to mean the slap or it's ineffective. Can't be the slightest hint you're playing with them."

She turns to me, pride in her eyes, "I usually get lots of compliments, thank yous, and free drinks from other women there. The guy will deride me for a moment, you ugly raging bitch, blah, blah, blah, trying to save his pride, but inevitably leaves the bar. I even got a standing ovation once." She rubs her knuckles against her chest in a 'damn right' gesture.

The half smile fades into a frown. She's looking at me intently, processing I suppose. "Well. That is worse than I imagined." She shakes her head, "I wasn't exaggerating though, somehow he forgave you years ago. Seems to me you need to forgive yourself, and maybe tell him just like you told me. It'll suck, but be done with."

Tentatively I scooch towards her, wanting comfort, "You make it sound so simple."

She puts her arm around me and I cuddle into her side, a bit of a role reversal for us. "It is simple Suzy. Ethan, you, me. Always. Now John too, I'm confident on that one. Do it."

Silently I nod, my heart pounding in my ears at the thought. She makes me feel safe though. Rachel's always sported a what's right is right approach, and now her confidence is leaking into me.

I kiss her lightly. "Ok." I pause. "Ok." Deep breath. "I can do it. Will you help?"

Giving me a squeeze, she rubs my shoulder gently and toys with my hair. "Of course Suzy, that's how friends work. Anything you need. Ultimately it's all inside you though."

Staring off towards the woods, I picture Ethan leaning against one of the trees. Noticing me, his face instantly absorbed by that goofy smile, he stands up straight and pushes away from the tree. Tossing something in the air he bats it my way, and I feel a fantasy peppermint land in my lap. He does a little jazz hands, eyebrows bouncing, silently mouthing 'Surprise!'

An imaginary me approaches, takes his head in both hands, 'I'm sorry Ethan. I'm so terribly sorry.'

No, that's not quite right. I close my eyes, and when I open them Ethan has his hand on the back of fifteen-year-old me. He pushes her towards adult me, away from the tree line. She is frightened, and stands tentatively, shoulders drooped and forward, trying to make herself smaller. Adult me does a little two-step at her, as if to say 'look what you turn into!' and she smiles shyly in return.

Adult me kneels slightly in front of young me, taking her shoulders in hand. 'You did a terrible, unforgivable thing, and we've punished ourselves for fourteen years now, uncertain how to deal with that. The only answer is to forgive anyway. It's time to let go.'

She pauses, straightens up. Looking down now she takes one cheek in her hand and gently tilts young me's face up. 'Suzy, I forgive you. I love you.'

Young me's eyes leak a little, the familiar stoic cry, and she nods. Then she pulls adult me into a sudden and aggressive bearhug. Just as abruptly she lets go and runs into the woods, smacking Ethan on the ass as she runs by.

He bursts out laughing. A joyful and exuberant release! Ethan and adult me hug each other, and she does a little shadow box at his belly.

Turning to Rachel and I on the porch, one arm around her, he lifts the other hand my way in a kind of salute, and with a rare closed mouth smile, eyes bright.

The fantasy fades away.

Sighing, I smile too. I can. I will.

5

We rock in silence for a while, processing both the terrible and the potentially amazing. The idea of reuniting with Ethan too, returning to the days of our inseparable threesome swims through me like warm water. Rachel's description of holding the idea close until she is full reverberates from my toes on up, making me ache with a desire I'd suppressed for years.

With a slight frown I remember that it'd be a foursome now. I'm uncertain how to feel about this exactly, no matter what kind of guy this John turns out to be. Worse, I'm not sure if he'd be the interloper. I have a feeling it'd be me.

I'm lying on my side now, with my head in Rachel's lap, and I reach behind me blindly, jostling a boob with the back of my hand. "Tell me about this John guy. Is he a goofball like me?"

Pushing my hand away, she rests hers on my head, lightly massaging my scalp. "Hm. Well, he's pretty silly, but not in the same way. Yours is more, I don't know, silly for silly's sake. It spills out of you without thought or design. John is just one of those dudes who revels in having zero shame. Anything for a good laugh. He responds to situations with the intent of being a goof, but not because he simply is one, like you. Does that make any sense?"

It doesn't. "I guess. Example?"

"Ok. Ah, so we all went to the grocery store. Ethan and John were roommates at the time, pooling money for things like that, and I'm in the next line over. Got to witness the whole thing anonymously. This poor twenty-something girl ringing them up casually asks if they're together, meaning the groceries. No doubt a question she asks all day, but something about the way John and Ethan interact, both pretty attractive dudes, and maybe a lack of interpersonal space, well she starts blushing and stammers, 'With the groceries I mean. Are your groceries together?'"

"John finds her thought and embarrassment instantly amusing, wraps his arms around Ethan's waist, kissing him wetly on the cheek and declaring 'Of course we're together! He's my little love muffin! Wouldn't you want to tear him apart every night?' Ethan plays along, pats John on the cheek and leans forward, placidly saying, 'the groceries are too.' The cashier smiles awkwardly but continues to be befuddled, fumbling through the process.

"As they're about to leave, a line of people behind him, John leans over the counter towards her, as if in confidence but loud enough for everyone to hear, 'You know, looking at us you'd think I'm the dominating force in bed, but that couldn't be further from the truth. He owns my body in unimaginable ways' shaking his head, 'I just can't even.' He's smiling distantly now, as if nostalgic, then turns back to her and comments, 'It's the quiet ones you've got to watch out for.'"

"I thought he'd gone too far, but he'd read her perfectly. Blushing fiercely now, that cashier leaned into him and whispered something right in his ear. He smiled at her for a moment, then gave her a big wink and a little fist bump, saying 'You go girl.'"

"Jovial, we both nearly tackled him outside! 'What did she say?' He gives us a belly laugh, wrapping his arms around both our shoulders and bringing us in close. Pausing right there in the parking lot, he closes his eyes, savors it, then finally whispers, 'I'm a quiet one too.'"

I turn on my back to look up at her and she's smiling broadly with the memory, not even the normal half smile.

I'm not sold. "Sounds a little obnoxious to me. People waiting in line and all."

She shrugs, "He gets away with it Suzy. Reads the whole crowd I guess. Has a lot of empathy, probably what makes him a good writer, and he wouldn't have pushed it so far if everyone around hadn't been chuckling. Shit, if there'd been some little old lady looking annoyed, he'd have focused on her instead. Charmed the pants off her. I've seen him do it!"

Draping her arm across my belly, she pinches me playfully. "It's always like that with him. He's just so damn friendly and confident. His sincere smile, his, I don't know, kind motives? He's always trying to include everyone. His size and good looks help too I guess. People instantly like him."

I'm still giving her a skeptical look, eyebrows furrowed.

She laughs, "You're a tough one! That would have won you right over if you didn't have this obvious jealousy raging away." She tries to tickle me, but I grab her hand.

Shaking her head, "Look, my favorite story is more wholesome. Just thought your dirty little mind would appreciate that one. Spur of the moment trip down to Charlotte for a pro basketball game. Apparently John played in high school with one of the visiting team guys. Ethan and I couldn't care less, but whatever, road trip."

I scoff a little and raise my eyebrows in mock, apt attention, "Oh? Do tell?"

Ignoring my jibe, "John gets those disgusting stadium nachos at the concession, and as we're turning to leave, this kid, eight or nine years old probably, trips a few steps ahead of us in the crowd. The kid had the nachos too, and his first thought was to cradle the container flat against his chest, to keep from spilling them right? and he somehow ends up lying on his back with the chips contained, but cheese goop, beans, meat, jalapenos, everything else, all oozing down both sides of his shirt towards the floor."

She snickers, "It looked like he'd been shot in a hokey action flick but had yellow blood and guts. Bursts out crying! His poor dad, standing there momentarily frozen, not knowing what to do while his kid's causing a scene. John didn't even hesitate! Plops down next to the kid, right on the gross stadium floor, leans back on an elbow and with a flourish smashes his nacho container against his chest. Wearing an expression of pure shock, he turns to face the kid!"

Now I am amused, and I sit up next to Rachel again, putting on her half smile.

She nudges me, glad to be grabbing my attention over her friend's story. "Right? Kid stops crying instantly, but just stares, confused. John raises his eyebrows, offering a 'watch this' expression. Sits up carefully and pulls out the bottom of his shirt, turning it up towards the nachos, exposing his belly but making a little bowl underneath the nachos like this." lifting the bottom of her shirt, miming the rest of the story while she narrates. "Releases the container, dropping it safely into the shirt bowl. Grabs a chip, dramatically brandishing it at the crowd that's stopped to watch the commotion, scoops some nacho goop right off his chest. Savors that chip like it's the best nacho ever! Mm, mm, mmm!" She does, in fact, look like she's just had the best nacho ever.

"Kid copies him exactly, all smiles now. They even toast chips like little beer mugs, right there on the floor."

I shake my head, bemused now. I do like this guy. Foursome huh? It's definitely too good to be true.

Rachel's watching my expression. "It was good Karma too. We helped John and the kid up, so they could protect their nacho shirt bowls, and he waved us off to find our seats so he could eat with the kid. Few minutes later he shows up wearing a new Hornets shirt and hands me a card. Kid's dad is a freaking literary agent. No. Shit. Only John."

She laughs again. I feel like I'm hearing about her boyfriend and I feel another, slightly odder, tinge of jealousy.

"He's still John's agent to this day! To be honest I don't think he'd even be published if he didn't have such a dedicated agent. Dude works his tail off for John."

Staring off into the trees, she's pensive for a moment, "Interestingly, John wasn't always like that. He was much more reserved when we all met. The jovial silliness simmered beneath the surface, but he was unable to permit himself to let go and be loose. Most of the time he'd simply smile and laugh quietly at any of Ethan's antics, vicarious I think."

Pausing a beat, "You know, you become like those you spend time with, and Ethan is never reserved, he is one hundred percent Ethan! I think he brought the real John out. His wholesome acceptance and goofy smile rubbed off on John in spectacular ways."

She tosses some fuzz from my shirt at the chipmunk, "Makes you appreciate just how formative the three of us were on each other as children, and truly marvel at what we had! John didn't have anything remotely like our depth of connection, and watching his friendship with Ethan grow, and then later becoming a part of it myself, well," Smiling, she looks back at me, "It was fascinating. Wonderful even! It was like seeing our childhoods play out all over again."

The chipmunk catches the fuzz, palms it between his paws, cocks his head at us. Seems to say, check me out. Tries to throw it, but it's caught in his claws. This, apparently, scares the poor little guy, and he starts flailing his paw and scampering around on the other three feet. Before I can even think how we might help him, he actually falls off the deck, vanishing from sight. I swear the shrill peep the robin makes is a laugh.

Getting up, I lean over the railing to see if he's ok, but before I can even look something gags me and a wave of dizziness, then nausea, runs through me like a freight train!

I stare at the trees and grip the railing, bracing and trying to stabilize my equilibrium, ignoring the sharp pain in my forearm. Seeing my distress Rachel is up next to me, and before I can think any further she's holding my hair as I wretch over the railing.

The world tilts impossibly once more, tossing me to the deck. My stomach still heaving weakly, Rachel frantically trying to help, I slump onto my side as my vision clouds, blackens. Dimly I hope I didn't puke on the chipmunk.

Taking a shallow breath, I feel calmer. Distantly, I sense Rachel. She's desperately speaking to me. Muted. It seems odd I can't hear her, but I can't find a reason to worry. She's here.

I reach forward and gently brush my fingertips against something. Not wood. Soft. A hand? I take it. Too rough to be Rachel's. Ethan? Oh, Ethan. I am so sorry!

Running my thumb across the back of the hand I feel wrinkles, paper thin. Gram? Tears springing up instantly, I struggle to sit up, to open my eyes against the blackness that's overtaken me. The light is brilliant and blinding!

Aghast, I grip her hand tightly as I relax back against the deck. Someone cradles my head. Rachel I suppose. I am remarkably comfortable, and a profound sense of peace swallows my tears.

I smile lightly, exhale a long, slow breath, and allow the blackness to overtake me.

6

I wake to the dim light of evening, Rachel sitting on the edge of the bed watching me. Seeing my eyes open she strokes my hair lightly. Eyebrows furrowed, she whispers, "Well hello sunshine. How do you feel?"

Sitting up on my elbows, I pull her hand away from my hair. She looks beautiful. "I feel pretty good actually. Did you brush my teeth?"

She laughs heartily, her shoulders visibly unknotting. Makes me laugh too of course, breaking the tension.

"That's your first question? Do you actually think I'd brush your teeth while you're unconscious?"

I smile awkwardly, shrugging and smacking my lips, "I dunno. I taste like mouthwash. I thought it was weird too, but remarkably considerate!"

Shaking her head at me, she smirks, "Well that's a lovely aftertaste for the foul goop you spewed out there." She shudders. "I had PB&J's for lunch. Apparently you had some kind of yellow baby food."

Cringing, I shove her off the bed, getting up to go brush my teeth. "Ugh! Thanks. I was feeling ok, but now you're making me nauseous again."

Staring into the mirror, I hardly recognize this person. She looks haggard, disheveled, scared. I spit into the sink with disgust. My usual spark is absent. I feel vacant. What the hell is going on?

It's time to admit it. I am not ok. Leaning forward, placing both hands on the sink, that shooting pain goes through my forearm again. I look it over. No marks. Shaking my head I squeeze the porcelain a bit, run my thumb over the cool metal border. I can't stand this confusion.

Looking back up, gripping the sink tighter, the air seems to warm perceptibly, like I'm having some kind of hot flash. I squinch my eyes shut tightly, bunching up my back and neck muscles with tension, and a suffocating sensation like the room is collapsing washes over me!

I pop my eyes open and suck in a huge breath. "Arrrgghhh!" I let it all out at my reflection.

Krrsssssssstk.

Startled, I watch the mirror shatter in slow motion, the cracks spidering in all directions at a leisurely pace, distorting my shocked expression into a Picasso.

Rachel comes in with my yell, stands there looking back and forth between me and the mirror, eyes wide. "Suzy, what the hell? Alfred is going to be pissed."

"I – I didn't touch it. I just yelled at it."

She gives me a 'yeah right' glare, but her expression melds into bewilderment as she grabs my wrist to move my hand, "Look!"

Clear as day, two handprints are firmly pressed into the sink and counter, wrapping around the edge to where my thumbs were. Gingerly I drag a fingertip along one of the indentions, a consistent half inch deep, hot to the touch. The handprints stretch across porcelain, the metal border, some kind of laminate counter, even into the top of the cabinet's wood under the right one. It's all rock solid.

Looking up at Rachel in astonishment, "They must have been there. That's crazy."

She turns my hand over in hers, as if expecting to see something magic. Looks normal. Gently places my hand into the grooves, an exact fit. I jerk my hand away, not wanting to see it slide in like a glove. And the heat - it almost burns.

Raising her eyebrows, I can tell she doesn't know what to say. A slow shrug instead, eyes still wide, shoulders keeping her ears company for a moment.

I echo the sentiment. Shake it off. There's simply some logical explanation we're missing. They were there. Coincidence of course. Alfred is one clever motherfucker.

Running my fingers through my hair I smooth it down, and Rachel hands me a clean shirt. We stare at each other in the fractured mirror for a moment, and I shake my head.

"Whew!" I say, turning to my reflection as I halfheartedly poke her on the nose, then poking several other noses in the Susan Picasso. "Whew. Whew. Whew." I can't bring myself to offer the usual 'suck it up buttercup' though.

"Fuck it. I need to sit down."

7

I plop down on the couch in the living room, across from the fireplace. Pretty comfy.

Rachel takes the other side, facing me Indian style, and wraps a blanket around her legs. She looks nervous. Timidly, she asks, "Well. What's going on? What happened out on the deck?"

I sigh, tired of this question bouncing around today. "I don't know. Just got really nauseous and dizzy all of a sudden."

She's quiet for a beat, then wraps her arms around her shoulders, in a little self-hug, and shivers slightly like she's cold. Looking over at the fireplace, she says, "It was scary. You nearly threw yourself to the deck, and I had to hold you on your side since you were still puking. Once you finished heaving you started muttering. Some kind of fit really, like in the movies. I couldn't understand anything except 'Gram'."

She shakes her head, a strand of hair falling into her face. "Even after you passed out I had to pry your hand off the bottom slat of the railing. Your grip was like a vice!"

"Gram? Jesus. My grandmother died when I was a child. I was ten or so I think."

I close my eyes, remembering the paper-thin feel of her hand the last time I held it, kneeling next to her while she smiled lightly at me from the lazy boy, smelling of mothballs. The hospice nurse suggested I share a story from school, and I told her how Ethan had started carrying peppermints for me. Gram mumbled 'peppermints' in response, and her eyes lit up a little. Died that night. The nurse knew it was coming I think.

Rachel leans forward onto her hands and knees, the blanket falling away, stretching across the couch to me. She pecks me on the nose, and presses her forehead against mine with her eyes closed.

"I thought that's who Gram was. I'd laugh it off if it didn't creep me out so much. This has been such a weird day, and whatever's going on with you seems neurological!" She opens her eyes, locking them with mine. "And now you're seeing the dead."

I scooch back slightly, pressing against the armrest, trying to smile reassuringly. God she doesn't even know I don't remember yesterday. I'd blow off her superstition and make fun of it, if only I didn't feel it too. I can't remember the last time I thought about Gram.

After a moment I decide belittling it is still the safest route, for my own benefit as much as hers. Trying to chuckle, "Don't get all superstitious on me! Just got her on the mind. This cabin makes me nostalgic."

Rachel frowns, nonplussed with my defensiveness, and slumps back into her spot against the other arm rest. "It is a little silly to worry about Gram I guess. Doesn't change the fact that something is going on. I couldn't rouse you for a solid five minutes, and even when I finally got you moving you were still incoherent." Looking at her watch, "Then you slept like a rock for nearly four hours! Shit, you didn't even move. I felt compelled to keep checking just to make sure you were breathing!"

She huffs, and shakes her hands like she's flinging something off her fingers. "That's horrifying Suzy. We need to get you to the ER."

I start to mumble something about how I'll feel better tomorrow, but then don't bother. She's right. "Ok. What's the plan?"

Knowing I would normally object, Rachel goes through about three expressions with my quick acquiescence, finally settling on determined with a touch of increased concern.

"Ok then. Well, we spent four days backpacking here, 30-ish miles, but we could make it back in two if you stay healthy enough to hike all day."

I can't hide my surprise to discover I've forgotten four days of backpacking. I try to play it off, but Rachel picks up on it instantly.

Sitting straight up and leaning towards me aggressively, "You didn't know that did you?" she accuses. "Jesus Christ, Suzy! Were you going to tell me? What's the last thing you remember?"

I shrug, looking away. "Getting ready for a run I guess. Sorta thought we day hiked here."

This scares me all the more, knowing we've got days to get to a hospital, and I slump down on the couch, scooching my butt towards Rachel so I can put my head on the armrest, and I throw both arms onto my forehead, over my eyes. "Fuck me." I mumble.

She takes my legs and stretches them into her lap, starting to rub my feet, trying to soothe. "It's going to be ok. You seem fine right now." Looking out the window, "No sense in leaving tonight, it's already dark. At first light tomorrow we'll get the hell out of here."

Sitting up on my elbows, "What about an emergency radio or something?"

Rachel shakes her head. "Shit I scoured this place while you slept. I was afraid you weren't going to wake up at all! Nothing. Found something else from Ethan and John though. Can't say I care at this point."

I'm more than happy to grab onto this diversion! "Oh god please distract me! What'd they leave?"

Pushing my feet off her lap, she gets up and grabs a log by the fireplace, apparently set aside by her earlier. Hands it to me. On one end, painstakingly drawn in pen, a triangle fills the space, each corner meeting the bark at the edge of the cut. It contains a multitude of progressively smaller triangles inside it, proportionately identical and carefully positioned into a repeating pattern, the smallest about half the size of a pencil eraser. It's rather beautiful in its symmetry and precision.

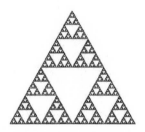

I look up at her, my face a question mark.

"It's a Sierpiński triangle, a classic example of a fractal."

I maintain my blank look, silently willing her to go on.

"Well it's not just any fractal, it's the one I put on the cover of my dissertation. Be a pretty fantastic coincidence if Ethan didn't draw that." She chuckles lightly, "John wouldn't have the patience."

My blank look morphs into a light bulb look, albeit a dim one. We have talked about this. "Right. A repeating pattern with all kinds of magic implications in mathematics."

She crinkles her eyes at me, her half smile fighting away the stress, then bops me on the leg. "Not just math my friend, fractals are all over nature. Think of a tree. Limb a repeat of the trunk, branch of the limb, twig of the branch. From seashells to snowflakes, lightning, mountainscapes, our nervous systems for Christ's sakes. Freaking broccoli! Fractals!"

Fully distracted now, she takes the log from me, admiring the Sepins-whatever triangle. "And the implications are enormous. We're just scratching the surface! Quantum physics, cosmology, biology, evolution, psychology, string theory, multiverses. Chaos theory! It all boils down to chaos theory!"

She actually places her hand on her chest, reverently, closing her eyes, "I've never felt such profound wonder as I did that first time I delved into chaos theory, stunned that something could explain so much while simultaneously opening an entire world of mystery. The growth of fractals from chaos answers some deep question I can't define and still don't know how to ask!"

Pausing a beat, she laughs, "Beauty from chaos, Suzy. Like me!"

Rachel looks a little wistful, mumbling, "Magic indeed." Gazing up blankly, she sends her half smile to the middle of the room. I actually look over to confirm she's staring at no one, which brings her back to me, amused.

Seeing her this engaged reminds me of childhood Rachel, and I'm both miffed that she seems to have completely forgotten the state of my brain and jealous that she's so passionately inspired by her work.

Realizing I'm glad this digression cleared the worry from her brow, I dismiss being miffed and try to encourage her. "Multiverse? Sounds like a videogame."

She laughs, "That one is a little out there. It's the idea that there are an infinite number of realities, or universes, but we're only conscious of the single one produced by our own series of choices. As in, each and every tiny choice you face leads to wholly different, yet fully formed and very real universes, and with your decision you are walking into one of them."

This makes my head hurt a little, "Jesus. What's the point of that thought exercise?"

Shrugging, "It's not a thought exercise if multiple, I mean infinite!, simultaneous realities really exist. It has implications for determinism, the meaning of time, consciousness, god." She has the log standing in front of her now, and is patting the triangle emphatically with each point. "It comes from quantum physics, where we have evidence of the same nano-particle being in different places at the exact same time. It's bizarre. And how is that possible? Multiverses! Ha!"

Wiggling her eyebrows at me, "And if the particle can access other versions of its multiverse, why can't we? Bum, bum, buuumm!" She jazz hands my way.

The room seems to wave a little, mirroring her gyrating fingers. I ignore it, and nod slowly. It is an intriguing concept, though I'd still lump it squarely into the thought exercise category.

Brushing dust off the log, she smiles up at me, "And you model this multiverse idea with what you ask? Ah, but of course you've already guessed, fractals!"

Holding the log towards me again, like a talisman, "Makes sense that Ethan would draw this too. We talked about the implications in psychology just last week and he loved it! He says our brains could be modeled as a fractal system, given the iterative processes they follow. The brain often uses repetition to solve problems, taking different paths each iteration, simplifying, seeking resolution. That's why we ruminate on mistakes, the brain is trying to resolve it and make us feel better. Patients with OCD get stuck in an iterative feedback loop that has no end, a glitch in the process. He was excited to discuss how fractals might impact neuro modeling or patient counseling with his adviser this week. Fractals for the win!"

I'm pretty sure I can't hear the word fractal again. "Well, you've officially blown my mind Brainiac." I hold both hands up in a stop gesture, "Now I know there's a universe where I didn't drink any water after puking, and we discussed fractals, iterative feedback loops, and general science magic well into the night, but in this universe I really need to pee."

She smiles a little ruefully, and slaps me on the ass as I walk by.

Safe in the bathroom, I desperately try to ignore the cracked mirror, and worse, the handprints staring at me from the sink.

8

Rachel's making a fire, though the math triangle log is displayed awkwardly on the bookshelf, hopefully forgotten.

I sit quietly on the couch, closing my eyes and listening to the quaint and comforting sounds of her stacking tinder and striking matches. Eventually I hear the gentle crackle of the fire.

Feeling the need to balance the room's brainpower at least a little, I try to contribute an intelligent sounding comment, "I get it I think. The multiverse is like the butterfly effect, except every possible outcome actually exists in its own separate reality."

"Right. The butterfly effect theory speaks to everything being so connected that a butterfly choosing to flap her wing on the other side of the planet could have profound effects on us, through an endless chain of cause and effect. The multiverse advocate would elaborate, saying her choice would also create multiple universes, new realties branching off in all directions based on the way she was facing, or the speed of her flap, the angle to the ground." She winks at me. "Nice analogy."

Smiling, I push my luck, "And from Ethan's psych perspective, the brain's iterative process could be a type of multiverse in itself. Like you said, taking different paths each iteration, it's making small changes to its own, internal universe, taking a peek at potential effects, seeking resolution to the problem."

She looks a little doubtful, as though I've crossed some imaginary line of plausibility. "You're speaking metaphorically, as a way to conceptualize the brain's mental process, instead of considering the literal idea of parallel universes." Shrugging, "But I suppose that's exactly what he was saying."

After a moment she dismisses her skeptical look and raises her eyebrows at me, "Maybe you and Ethan should get together to discuss it."

There's a brief, pregnant pause, but suddenly she starts giggling lightly, and plops into my lap on the couch. "Oh my god, sorry for the tangent, but did I ever tell you about the butterfly handjob?"

Amused, I shake my head no, marveling at how much better I feel. Our easy comradery is all I really want in life. And her laughter. Oh, so many times over, her laughter! I feel a little teary at the thought, but suppress them lest I derail this new direction. I am definitely hoping 'butterfly handjob' isn't some weird metaphor. I'd be relieved if I successfully asserted some intelligence only to then ditch Rachel's dorky math world for something more concrete. Nothing like a good sex story to bring this back to my level!

She's still giggling, and takes a deep breath, eyes alight. "I try to toss it into casual conversation with Ethan whenever I get the chance! He blushes every. Single. Time! And still hasn't come up with a clever response. Spectacular."

Laughing again, she lays down on her back, looking up at me with her head in my lap, "Did you know he and I practiced that little scene I made up for you over and over?"

Now it's my turn to laugh, "Oh man. No! You're kidding."

"Not at all. I wanted it perfect. I knew it was a long shot, and was hellbent on knocking your socks off, and your pants for that matter." She shakes her head, mocking, "Poor ol' Ethan. Seventeen-year-old boy hormones running wild, hadn't touched a girl since you, about two years by then, and this tight little body is rubbing up on him." Pointing at herself with an exaggerated gesture, like she's kidding though we both know she's not.

"Ha! If it weren't so hypocritical I'd feel jealous, though I'm not sure of who! I can't believe you two were making out!"

Squinching her eyes shut tightly, she nods heartily with little huffs sputtering through her nose. "Yeah, he couldn't either!"

She calms a little, sits up next to me. "Despite being pretend, it was some serious intimacy and we'd definitely lose ourselves in it. We were both embarrassed the first time I was between his legs, pulling him into me like Steve supposedly did, and his dick was rock hard against my hip. He blushed fiercely and we both started laughing! I was all like 'I hope that doesn't happen with Suzy!' but I took it as feedback that the scene was working, and your stand-in having an inappropriate bulge just became part of it."

"He'd always stop it about the time I climbed into his lap though, making it into a joke, grabbing his chest and shaking it at me, or putting my hands there instead and yelling 'Take me Rach! Ravish me! I am your flower to plunder!' or something. You know Ethan."

I do. I can totally picture that. I laugh appreciatively, enthralled to find out where this is going.

"Well, the week before that party, I'd already decided it was time to go for it with you and I didn't want the scene to stop anymore. I wanted a full-on dress rehearsal, so to speak! We were practicing, and as soon as I caught the look in Ethan's eye, that he'd had enough, I took evasive action! He went to grab my hands to make some joke, and I grinded into him harder, biting his lip gently and taking his hand instead, guiding it onto my breast. He popped it back off like my tit was some kind of hot potato, but I'd dodged the joke and sent us into new territory, his expression a mess of confusion and desire, uncertainty."

She rubs the back of her neck, looking uncertain herself, "I guess I took advantage of him a little, but we both wanted it, just for different reasons. I mean, we loved each other." She shrugs. "And, well, I wanted to thank him too, in a slightly misguided teenage way. Anyway, I leaned into his ear and whispered 'It's ok Ethan, I want it' and then I leaned back, locked eyes with him and took my shirt and bra off."

I shake my head, astonished at this scene, and then chuckle a little, wondering if that was the first time Ethan saw bare breasts. I'd kept my bra on. Not to mention mine aren't that much to look at.

She raises her eyebrows, laughing with a small grimace, "Well he didn't need any more encouragement after that! So we made out for a while, and I've got to say I was proud he was so much gentler with my breasts than other guys I'd been with. Eventually I scooched back, just like with you, undid his pants and pulled out little Ethan. Didn't take long from there. Made a terrific mess!"

"He was a little awkward after, wanting to go clean up, but I hushed him and held him a minute. I just wanted to hang on to the intimacy a little longer you know? Eventually I leaned back and took his hand, guiding it and offering pointers on how to touch breasts and nipples, laughing together at how sticky we were. I liked the idea of helping him with girls in a way only I could, as a friend."

Raising her eyebrows with a little head tilt, she shrugs. "Changed the dynamic of our relationship for sure, for the better though, opening up a whole new arena of conversation. Shit I've given him all kinds of blunt pointers and sex advice over the years!"

It never ceases to amaze me how bold and confident Rachel has always been. I still can't imagine telling someone, 'Hey, here's how you should touch my breasts.' and here she is at seventeen without even thinking twice about it.

"So why was it the 'butterfly handjob?'"

She laughs, bopping herself on the forehead lightly, "Right! I spaced on the whole point of the story! I was pretty devastated after you."

I interrupt with a quiet, "Oh, Rach!" but she waves this off.

"And I met up with Ethan at the oak to talk about it." She gets quieter, darker, "I just needed comfort you know? But he was mad for some reason! Actually yelling at me, despite my tears over you. I couldn't understand it, or believe it, and suddenly my whole world was collapsing around me. I went from tears feeling sorry for myself to a complete snotty mess. I grabbed his arms to shake him, and at my touch, something, I don't know, changed in him. I could see it go through his eyes. As swiftly as it came his anger was gone, and he softened. Wiping the snot from my face with his sleeve, he tucked my hair behind an ear and said, 'Rach, maybe you're not gay.'"

I put on a face of disbelief, and Rachel laughs.

"Right? Fucking teenage boy hormones completely obscuring logic! In retrospect it's easy to see from his perspective I suppose. He and I share this great moment of intimacy, monumental for him I think, and then it doesn't go well with you, well clearly he and I should be together!"

Shaking her head again, "I mean my magic fingers worked on a guy and not a girl! Well, despite being a horrible bawling mess only moments earlier, I laughed right in his face. Yup. A disbelieving, hurt, but hearty laugh! A release really. And then he starts chuckling, abashed, and apologizes for being angry before. The tension gone, mood completely remedied, we got down to the business of him holding me under that oak while I cried over you."

She shudders. "Afterwards, it was painfully obvious our recent intimacy had redirected his hopeful, teenage brain, and that I might have lost him if I hadn't done it! I can't even imagine where my life would have gone if I'd lost both my best friends simultaneously."

She's staring at the fire, "I was actually planning to go to a basketball party that night, make the scene real with Steve."

I grimace, and she looks back at me, "Yeah, what a terrible move that would been! He was a real meathead. Ethan wouldn't let me though. Took me out to Figaro's instead."

Her face softens, eyes wet, "Over pizza I said I almost lost him under that oak, and he didn't even argue! Simply shook his head sadly, apologizing again. My god." She pauses a beat. "Said he felt this sort of blind rage until the idea that he and I belonged together occurred to him. That he was ashamed and terrified of what he might have done if I hadn't put the idea there in the first place."

We're both quiet a moment, then she giggles lightly, smirking up at me. "It's all the more bizarre since giving my best friend a handjob was such an unlikely scenario. I knew I was a lesbian by then." She shakes her head, mumbling, "Crazy."

She blows out some air, a release. "So, yeah, I dubbed it the 'butterfly handjob' because a small, albeit sweet and intimate, gesture ended up having a monumental impact on my life! The butterfly effect in action!"

Smiling at me again, shaking off the notion of losing both her best friends, "Plus at first he joked about how he needed more boob training, and my comeback that I couldn't risk the awesome power of another butterfly handjob effectively silenced that notion!"

Placing her hand on my chest, she looks me deep into the eyes, oozing mock sincerity, "Ethan, it's simply too dangerous! Next time there'll be a disruption in the space-time continuum, a wormhole opened in Asia, reversal of the magnetic fields, the sky itself could fracture!"

Taking her hand away, raising them both, eyes wide with apparent fear, "I am not getting anywhere near your magic penis!"

Laughing I take her hands, "Bringing it out had a pretty profound effect on my relationship with him too. That thing is dangerous! How on Earth do you work that into casual conversation?"

"Oh you know, anytime something needs to have a profound effect, like you said! Say hanging at a bar with friends."

She stands up, miming an exciting conversation, with exaggerated hand gestures and alternating a higher pitched voice with her own.

"How's your dissertation coming Rach?"

"Oh it's EPIC! My committee: minds blown!" Making exploding motions on either side of her head, complete with sound effects, then crossing her arms. "Believe it or not, it's even more powerful than my butterfly handjob!"

"Uh, ok. What the hell does that mean?"

"You don't know? Ethan can explain." Casually pointing a thumb to her left, as if Ethan's standing there.

"He always blushes, laughs a little uncomfortably and changes the subject, while I offer the group surprise and confusion at his reaction, ensuring someone jibes him a little, trying to get the story. Never ceases to amuse!"

Looking at her smile, the twinkle in her eyes at the memory, I can't help but feel a little melancholy over all the years I've missed with the two of them. I could have been part of this casual intimacy with my best friends, instead of growing increasingly reclusive in my little mountain home out west, trees, a cat and a laptop for company.

Staring at the fire, for a moment I imagine my home burning, Samson streaking out of a window and into my arms. Rachel and Ethan by my side, both with an arm around my shoulders, silent, watching. I blink and add their friend John leaning against a tree, eating some nachos.

9

After dinner we crawl into bed, glad to be approaching the end of an exhausting day. Rachel playfully scooches back against me, pulling my arms around her, making me into big spoon. It's a good fit. I take in the comfortable smell of her hair, let it envelop me a bit. Revel in the human contact of my best friend.

She presses her butt against me lightly, a subtle invitation, a natural reaction to the closeness of a lover, and one I wish I shared. Most of our sex life has included at least a few beers for me, a fact I'm embarrassed about.

I close my eyes, trying to find the denial I've been operating under these last few months. I've finally achieved some of the emotional intimacy I ache for, but at what price? I am using my body to get it. I am using her. I do not love her in the way she loves me, and I'm increasingly certain I never will.

As always, I remind myself that I do love her, as my friend, confidant, partner in crime. Our laughter, the comfort and peace it brings me! Goddamnit, I love everything about her and us, except actually being her lover! I know I've been rationalizing it, but surely this decision is common even when the body parts match the desire, if everything else is great. I refuse to accept that I can't have this emotional comfort simply because the puzzle pieces don't fit in the way some animalistic part of me craves.

I sigh. My body objects. My brain tends to agree. Worst of all, I'm deceiving her. Guilt overpowers me.

Something about the day. Partly fear. I mean, what's wrong with me? What if I'm actually dying or something?! Partly just being with Rachel, experiencing the brave, confident way she's handled my confusion and sickness. I don't know. But I do know I can't deceive her anymore. Whatever this is between us, I know playing pretend isn't right. My eyes try to leak as I set my jaw.

I take a deep breath, squeezing her a little, "Rachel?"

"Mmm?"

"Rachel, I'm," I pause, terrified to lose her touch, squeezing her tighter. "I'm not gay."

She tenses for a moment, freezing in place, but then relaxes back into me, stroking my forearm lightly. "I know." She says quietly.

I'm not sure what to say. "I, uh, ok. That doesn't bother you?"

She turns over in my arms to lay on her back, and I sit up on an elbow looking down at her. She's searching my face.

After a moment, her half smile is in place. "I wouldn't choose it." Poking me teasingly, "I've certainly had better sex. I keep hoping I'll find the key that unleashes the beast Oliver knew, but that enthusiasm belongs to the right man I guess."

Blushing fiercely, I try to focus my embarrassment on the idea of Oliver, but it doesn't work. I'd never thought about her perspective on our sex life. Of course it's not that great for her either! I think of some of the men I've been with who weren't really there. Not enthused about me or maybe my body, closing their eyes in such a way I know they're fantasizing about someone else, simply trying to get to the release. Might as well be using my body to masturbate. I'm ashamed to realize that's what I've given Rachel! Oh god.

I feel the immediate need to defend my sexual prowess and prove the notion wrong, but of course I don't really want to. You can't simply invent the desire out of thin air.

She puts a hand on my chest, between my breasts. "It's ok Suzy. Believe me, if I had a bottle of Oliver's pheromones I'd douse myself nightly! Shit, I was at this creepy thrift store with Ethan the other day, absolutely packed with old useless junk, and we found this ornate blue vial. We were joking that's what was in it, and that I needed to harness its fearsome effect. Ethan even bought it."

I frown lightly, laying down next to her so we're both facing the ceiling. "Well I'm glad to hear Ethan knows I suck at being a lesbian too."

She laughs and smacks my hip with the back of her hand, saying nothing.

Relieved to have been honest, but trying to change the subject before we start discussing what that means for us, I grab the handiest tangent. I've been avoiding the question, but now that I'm planning to own my mistakes with him, it seems safer. "So how is Ethan anyway? Is he happy?"

Rachel takes my hand and holds it down by her hip. It's an unassuming gesture that could mean friend or lover, comfortable and perfect in its ambiguity, a reassurance that we're friends first. I'm sure we'll have to address it more later, but she knows I'm not up for that tonight. I doubt she is either.

"He is. Loves his psych program, going to be a wonderful therapist someday, if he'll get his shit together and knock out his dissertation anyway. Been dating Anne for a few years now. We hang out a lot, and she's cool. In his psych program too, super intelligent, fun. Attractive in a quirky way, sorta like he is in fact. A good fit for him I think." She shrugs, "Doesn't shave her pits though. Pretty weird, especially for a straight girl."

Giggling, "I didn't know that was a lesbian thing! Maybe it would help me if I stopped shaving?"

Rachel laughs too, "Please don't! God, Josie didn't shave anything and it was too much for me. I brought it up once and she went full on fema-nazi on me. I'm not certain what the patriarchy had to do with her body hair, but apparently it was important to defy them!"

She shakes her head, a wisp of hair tickling my nose and I have to scratch. "Ethan was clearly uncomfortable with Anne's at first, even commiserating with me over Josie's, but now he says it's sexy and exotic. He's proud of it, in a way, an emblem of her confidence maybe." She's quiet a beat, then muses, "I did like Josie's sometimes, when I was really hot for her. I used to think it was simply Pavlovian, but in retrospect I know it was more than that. It all comes down to pheromones Suzy."

I don't say anything, allowing myself to remember Oliver, and compare that desire to other men I'd been with. It's not like he did anything special in bed. If anything, he used me more than most others.

Now it's her turn to sit up on an elbow, looking down at me. "I've thought about my sexuality a lot over the years. It certainly hasn't been the easiest path to follow, and I absolutely didn't choose it! All this nonsense people spout about nature or nurture, arguing over choice in orientation. The only choice is whether to deny our base desires or not!"

She pauses, collecting her thoughts. "Look, the sexuality of the entire animal kingdom is driven by pheromones, we're not any different. Processing smell is one of our deepest brain functions, taking place in the limbic system, in the brain stem!

An area also driving emotions, survival instinct, hormonal regulation, all directly related to sexuality."

Gazing out the window now, addressing someone else with a slight plea, her parents maybe, "Sexual orientation is determined by pheromones. It just makes sense. It's horrible not to accept that."

Laying back down with a huff. "Sorry about the soapbox, but it pisses me off. I'm wired to be attracted to women! The deepest part of my brain senses female pheromones and says go! I didn't choose it any more than you chose men." She sniffles a little. "From that light it's all the more meaningful that you've wanted to date me, despite the way you're wired."

I don't know how to respond to this soliloquy, laced with implications about us, but I share her little surge of emotion. Oh Rachel, why is it so complicated? Eyes wet, I roll over and lay my arm across her belly, and after a moment's hesitation, throw my leg over hers and kiss her neck, nuzzling in. Bends the friendship barrier a bit, if that's where we're heading, but it feels good and I don't care. I'm not sure where all these lines are, between comfort, love, and sex. Everything is one big grey area anyway.

Sliding her arm under my neck, she squeezes me tight, then strokes my side and back for a few minutes. We lay there in a companionable silence, lost in thought over a weighty day. Before I know it I feel her breathing slow, deepen.

I'm not tired, having slept, been unconscious, or whatever that was, all afternoon, and can't fall asleep. Carefully I sneak out of bed and cover her up. She rolls over, but doesn't seem to wake.

Grabbing the blanket Rachel had on the couch, I wrap it around my shoulders and walk outside. The sky is clear, no moon, no light pollution, and the stars are absolutely brilliant. I mean, Breathtaking! Not wanting to make any noise with the porch swing, I simply sit on the stairs to the deck, looking up. I breathe deep, taking it in.

I wish tomorrow wasn't hiking, and that it would bring answers instead, but at least we have a plan. I feel fine right now, and the hospital will come soon enough.

I examine my forearm, poking and prodding until I find the exact spot. There's just one area, but it covers the width of my arm and is quite sharp, though for the first time I note my wrist hurts in a few places too. I must have fallen, banging my forearm and maybe breaking my fall with my hand. Surely I hit my head too though. I smile. The simplest explanation. Occam's Razor.

I feel small looking up at the stars, and wonder if I want answers at the hospital. A CT reveals a brain tumor, then what? But if the CT is clean, what does days of amnesia mean? Vertigo, mystery pains, sudden, violent nausea? What else, hallucinations maybe? Rachel definitely looked like someone else this morning! Could a concussion cause all that? Oy.

If I do have a tumor, if I'm actually dying, what would I do differently? Reconcile with Ethan. One hundred percent. Probably move back home to be closer to everyone. I'm not certain Rachel and I will keep dating, I doubt it I guess, but I can't lose her again. After tonight's confession, it's clearly too much to ask her to go through with moving out west. That ship has sailed, thankfully I suppose, since it's not too late. It pains me to think of my leaving Montana instead, but that's the solution. I've been running away, and I don't want to be a recluse anymore. I sigh.

Stealthily grabbing a cushion off the swing, I tiptoe off the deck and lay down, wrapping up in the blanket. I don't think I'd actually wake Rachel from out here, but I feel compelled to make as little noise as possible, not wanting to disturb the serenity surrounding me, enveloping me!

Now I really have a view of the sky, the nearby trees and roof of the cabin black against the stars. The milky way is easy to make out, and it only takes a few minutes to spot a shooting star.

Feeling content, and a bit less scared, I sigh again, longer, almost a balloon deflating. I suppose the point of that thought exercise is to realize the future is always unknown, never guaranteed, ultimately life is short, and I should do all these things either way.

Ok brain, I've had my revelation! Now it's time to find out I don't have a tumor, and discover how I got such a severe concussion. I offer the Milky Way Rachel's half smile, and try to feel hopeful.

I lay that way for a long time, realizing I'm drifting off but unwilling to go back inside. My mind wanders to stargazing out in our field.

In our early teens Rachel and I would tell our parents we were staying at each other's houses, with Ethan taking advantage of divorced parents who hated each other, each making an easy alibi for the other. Freed us up to camp by that oak together. We'd set up a tent in case it rained, but lay out in the field where we could see the entire sky, a fluffy comforter under our sleeping bags.

Spending the evening telling stories, jokes, complaining about our families or school, all the while sharing candy or even a beer one of us pilfered from our parents, it was always magical, and we never got caught!

As the night wore on we'd get deeper, making plans for the future, exploring our hopes, truly letting our imaginations run free and feeding off each other's dreams. Eventually we'd quiet down, staring up, mesmerized by the vast swath of stars shining down and lost in wonder.

Rachel was usually nestled against Ethan, her head on his arm, and I'd be pressed close to her, holding hands, all looking straight up. Much like Rachel and I were tonight actually. I smile lightly at the similarity. We should have come out here instead of going to bed!

A light breeze ruffles my hair. The muffled sound of a distant owl. At peace, sleep takes me, amongst the remembered warmth of my friends.

10

The dim light of dawn wakes me. Damp with morning dew, and stiff as hell, I sit up, pulling the blanket along with me, a barrier against the morning chill. Somehow I'm not surprised to see the chipmunk there watching, head cocked, relaxed back on his haunches, a sentry keeping track of my every move.

We stare at each other, and after a moment he does his grizzly bear routine, standing straight up, arms in the air, a nut in his right paw. Giving him a thumbs up, I take in the cabin, looking peaceful in the morning light, though I feel a twinge of guilt for leaving the door wide open.

I catch the silhouette of Rachel shuffling around inside, and after a moment I hear the homey sounds of putting on water for coffee. Up at dawn, neither of our norms! I stretch and sigh. She wasn't kidding about getting the hell out of here this morning.

Making a few light squeaky noises at the chipmunk, I try to greet him in his language, but he slowly sits back on his haunches in apparent confusion. I suppose my chipmunk-speak needs work. I shoo him away and trudge inside.

She looks a little hurt, and with a pang I realize of course she feels I rejected her by sleeping outside, especially right after flat out telling her I don't want her sexually.

Goddamnit! Careless. That's me, careless with my friends. When am I going to learn? After our weighty conversation last night, a little extra effort on my part was important. Nope, I'm just going to ignore you and do my own thing. Jesus, Suzy.

Still waking up, I'm standing in the door staring at her, shoulders slumped as I chastise myself. I shake it off and stand up straight. Throwing the blanket to the floor with a flourish, I start a little dance.

Her half smile pops up. It's clearly time for an over the top, improvised apology performance!

"I am. Bum, bum. So damn dumb! Bum, bum." A few little kicks.

"Can't believe. Bum, bum. I let you. Bum. Sleep a-lone!" Hands in the air, firework motions!

"Looked like. Bum, bum. I didn't care!" Shaking my boobs at her now.

"So far. Bum, bum. From the truth!" Boob shake, kick, boob shake!

"Can't believe. Bum, bum. I'm so uncouth!" Twirling slowly, arms out, head back.

"Fell asleep. Bum, bum. Looking at the view." Faster, big finish now.

"Surrounded. Bum, bum. With thoughts of you!" Down on one knee. Jazz hands!

She laughs and helps me up, right into a bear hug. "Didn't read much into it actually. Just scared me, you know? not knowing where you were when I woke up. With everything going on…" She shrugs, the thought trailing off.

She lets go and pushes me lightly on the shoulder. "Did you try to rhyme 'dumb' and 'alone' though? I don't think I can let that slide."

I smile ruefully, laughing. "I thought it was pretty damn good on the spot! Shit, it's like five AM or something for Christ's sakes."

Handing me my Hello Kitty coffee, "No excuse. A girl's got to have standards."

⇜⇝

Backpacks packed, full to the brim again and weighing us down, we're standing in the yard looking back at the cabin. We gathered the used sheets and all the towels into a pile, but it seems lazy.

"I feel guilty Rach. This place was amazing and we're leaving it a mess. Shouldn't we wash everything in the sink and hang them to dry or something?"

She looks pensive, studying the cabin. "Maybe. We're not though. We're moving." She tousles my hair absently, then rests her hand on the back of my neck, taking the cabin in for another long moment. "Alfred will understand."

Turning, she begins to push her way down the trail through the overgrowth. "Come on."

I know we need to leave, but something doesn't feel right. I'm suddenly frightened, and can't shake the notion that I won't make it through the woods. This is the only thing I remember out here, and it feels like a safe haven. Telling myself how silly that is, I turn to follow Rachel, and the robin takes off a few feet in front of me! I hadn't seen him there in the grass, and I turn back to the cabin, following his flight. He lands on the sign over the door.

'You Are Welcome'. It feels like a nice gesture of farewell, or maybe of 'don't go', and I raise my hand slowly, offering a solemn goodbye. I stop though, leaving my hand stranded about halfway up, noticing light leaking out around the edges of the door. I start to head back to turn off the lights, when I remember there's no power.

Dropping both hands to my side, I stand there dumbfounded for a moment, staring and trying to process the glowing lines around the doorframe.

They're growing, thickening. The smooth line of the door now ill defined, wavy. I take a step back as the light bleeds across the surface of the door, the consistency of lava, but bright white, dribbling, streaking, picking up speed.

A flash blinds me and I yelp! It hurts, my pupils too dilated for it, like a sudden picture taken in the dark. With my hand up against the blinding light I try to peer through my fingers, heat streaming at me across the yard! There's a figure in the doorway!

"R-Rach?" I stammer, much quieter than I intended.

The light bleeds from the doorway onto the cabin in tendrils like white flames, and the figure is black against this backdrop, my eyes unable to focus. Is it reaching out?

"RACHEL!?"

I scream as she grabs my pack from behind, spinning me into her arms!

She holds me tight, stroking my head, soothing. Quietly murmuring, "It's ok. It's ok. It's ok."

Still in her arms, awkwardly gripping her backpack in an attempted hug, I turn my head back to the cabin. The light is gone, but so is the door. No one there. The doorframe appears burned, and I can't even read the sign from here, which looks thoroughly blackened.

Rachel pulls away and looks at me, then over at the cabin, then back at me. Her expression is hard to read, a mix of fear, confusion, anger. "What the fuck?" astonished, quiet.

Mute, I gesture expansively, emphatically towards the cabin and the gaping hole of a door.

Still stroking my hair lightly, Rachel scowls at the cabin. "Wha? Uh. The-The propane? I didn't hear anything."

Squinching my eyes shut tightly, I pull her closer. I feel Rachel's heartbeat against my chest, hard, fast, a comfort. I keep seeing the figure, it was reaching towards me! Plaintive!

I snap my eyes open, focusing on all the normal, real things around me. The trees, the weight of my pack, Rachel's warmth, her presence. I silently count thirty of her heartbeats, quieting, slowing as we calm together. Taking a deep breath, I focus on slowing my breathing too. Rachel.

"Propane." I whisper.

Fuck this. I am out. With an angry huff I push her off me. One good, full-body shudder, and I stomp off ahead down the trail.

11

We hike in silence, neither of us daring to address the imploding cabin door. Some mysterious physics associated with propane. I'm no propane expert! Everything else a figment of my overactive imagination. Clearly. Smiling bitterly, I realize or of my brain tumor. No comfort there, but maybe it's better than an actual demon/beast/zombie? I shake my head.

Let's stick with the imagination theory. Right. Know what? I'm going to assume that was friendly, plaintive. Like, 'Hey, I've got a flat tire.' Or 'Hey Suzy, have you read *Watership Down*? It's my favorite book! Let's make hot cocoa and read together. Wait, come back!' Yes. Now there's imagination to the rescue. Nodding to myself, I mentally thank the figure, 'Oh, that's very kind, but I simply must get moving. It's my brain you see.' Ok. Rachel's probably wondering why I'm pointing at my head.

Looking about me, another deep breath, and I realize I do feel better. The power of directing your focus onto something positive. The cabin is history, and the trail is lovely. Moving on, moving on. I try to admire the trees. I smile.

Stopping for a second, I turn and bop Rachel on the arm. The half smile pops right up! Kind eyes, understanding. We hike on.

There's nothing but smooth, easy trail, lined by trees, and we cruise. Before I know it the forest falls away as we come around a corner, revealing a rocky outcropping next to a cliff.

Rachel stops, looking uncertain. "This is where that picture was taken." Wiping the sweat from her face, she walks over to the outcropping, looking around. "I don't understand. There haven't been any side trails, but I don't think we came this way. I'd have recognized it before."

I shudder. The last thing we need is to get lost. "Maybe it's not as obvious coming from the other direction?"

Hesitantly, she walks the tree line and I follow her around the bend. The trail continues beside the cliff. She pauses, then stomps a little ways out, then stops again, puts her hands on her hips.

She's glaring at the trail, looking over the cliff, and I take a moment to enjoy the view. Rolling hills, green with nothing but trees. Distant, larger mountains, but not the Rockies. Oregon, I think, maybe Washington.

Something doesn't fit. "It's so strange not to remember, but I assumed we were in the Blueridge somewhere, back home, not out West."

Rachel side-eyes me. "We are. You think Ethan and John flew cross country to plant a picture and a drawing on a log?"

Right. That's what didn't fit. I put my hands on my hips too, watching her study the trail and cliff. After a moment I punch her on the shoulder. She looks up at me, annoyed, and I jab my finger towards the big mountains. The big, snow-capped mountains.

Her jaw drops, shoulders sag. Rachel stares.

As the one here with memories of the trip, she needs to explain. I wait a beat, then finally prompt, "I'm no mountain expert, but I'm pretty sure there's nothing like that in Appalachia."

"Maybe in the Northeast." She murmurs, still staring.

I huff. "Are we in the Northeast?"

"No."

She seems frozen in confusion. I can't decide if I'm angry, scared, or relieved to have company in the general state of disorientation I've been enjoying. Welcome to my world Rach! Soon neither of us will remember!

I look for a place to take off my pack, but the trail is narrow, with nothing but a rock wall on one side and scree leading to the cliff on the other. I try to stretch my shoulders while I watch her process, the gears in that big logical brain spinning like mad, looking a little off their tracks. Raising my eyebrows in her general direction, I wait for the gears to find something productive.

I don't have to wait long. Suddenly she shakes her hands out, runs fingers through her hair and stands up straighter. "I picked you up at the Charlotte Airport. We're just outside Asheville." Setting her jaw, she gestures at the view, "An unusually heavy snowstorm in the mountains, and those must be closer than they look, so they're not so big. It's just strange seeing them with so much snow this time of year."

On the plausibility scale that's about a zero, but I'm hardly in a position to argue about where we are. She stares at the mountains another moment, then grunts, shrugging. Her shoulders relax and I can see she's sold herself on it. "Ethan and I got flurries hiking Mount Mitchell in the summer a few years ago, so heavy storms must happen in the fall sometimes."

I don't say anything, but I'm squinting at her wondering if a gear did run off the track. She does a double take my way, then bursts out laughing, squinting back at me, which of course makes me laugh.

We're both giggling when I notice, and point, laughing harder, at a chipmunk in the trail doing a fine imitation of the cabin chipmunk, nut in paw, grizzly bear and all.

After thinking that, I have to say it aloud, "Nut in paw, grizzly bear and all!" making Rachel snort, which in turn escalates our giggle fest into full on belly laughs!

Eyes watering, jelly legs making me put a hand on her pack for support, I start to get nervous on the narrow trail and try to shake it off, pursing my lips and blowing out in huffs.

The chipmunk flings the nut about ten inches to his left. He's chittering like a madman, and starts striding towards us, upright!

Rachel blinks once, then channels her high school days playing soccer, kicking that chipmunk a solid thirty feet off the cliff!

Shocked, still trying to get ahold of myself, "Rach! What the? You just murdered that chipmunk!"

She stares out after him for a moment, then turns to me with a satisfied frown, "Still got it. That was left footed too." She pauses a beat, taking in my shocked expression, "What? That was creepy as hell. He was running at us upright! Probably rabid or something."

Wiping the tears out of my eyes, I chuckle one more time, bemused, "Shit, he was probably just pissed we were laughing at him!"

Smiling at me, she leans in and pecks me on the lips, mumbling, "This trip cannot get any stranger."

Refocusing, she massages her shoulders a moment, spending a few seconds looking in each direction.

Finally she gestures on down the trail, along the cliff. "I'm certain we didn't miss a turn, it has to be this way. Let's get out of here."

Turning to go, suddenly there's a 'thwock' and the hair on one side of her head bounces up. She stumbles forward as I process that something hit her! I grab her pack from behind, to stop her from stepping into the scree.

Too late! She's sliding! Falling to my knees on the trail, I use every muscle I have to create leverage. There isn't any! I'm pulled out and sliding behind her. I slump to my side, trying to cradle her pack against me as lightning pain shoots through my forearm, then numbness below the elbow.

Her pack is wrenched out of my remaining arm as she tumbles over the edge! I slide off right behind her.

Somehow, I'm not really surprised. Time seems to slow and I find we're facing each other as we fall, her pack towards the ground, hair streaming up towards me, whipping around her face in the wind. Me, head first just behind.

We try to join hands but can't quite reach. The robin sits in her hair placidly, tangled, not even trying to fly, a tiny robin-shaped balloon tied to her ear.

First, I'm reminded of this ride at the fair when we were children. We were spinning, facing each other, her hair reaching out to me just like now. We shrieked hysterically the entire time!

That memory doesn't fit though. No shrieking today. Her expression now a little sorrowful, but so full of love I catch my breath. Actually, I'm certain it's the expression I never saw, but imagined countless times over the years. The one she wore when I left her on that couch, after we made out as teenagers. No expectation, only acceptance. Of me. Of everything that is Susan. Tinged with loss, but not sadness. Something expansive shining in her eyes that swallows up any sorrow, fear, vulnerability. Something that aches, but only because it longs to be shared and it's too big to ever fully do so. Something... Perfect.

I close my eyes, try to recapture the feeling. I had drunkenly paused at the door, stunned, doorknob in hand. A moment of decision still frozen in time. And I walked out. I did not look back. Yes, awoken behind me, she had sent a love letter, stamped, earnestly mailed, strawberry perfumed with the taste of her lips, complete with understanding, compassion and a plea, backed by ten years growing up together. All at once I had been overwhelmed with every laugh, every smile, the years culminating into something more than connection, her confusing desires as we moved into puberty, the way she looked at me as we whispered about boys, eventually love, LOVE, feelings blossomed unchecked throughout our inseparable and ideal friendship! She had rolled it all into a neat little package as she breathed my name.

I open my eyes. She smiles lightly, hair still whipping about her face. I know how she felt. Feels. I know.

"Rachel."

PART IV

And above all,
watch with glittering eyes the whole world around you
because the greatest secrets are always hidden
in the most unlikely places.
Those who don't believe in magic will never find it.

The Minpins, Roald Dahl

1

Breathe.

I glance about to find myself in a rickety cabin I explored as a child. Awash with memory, I can feel the magic and mystery invoked by that bright-eyed little girl. It was all around as I tentatively tiptoed, a treasure waiting in every closet, behind every book, under a secret floorboard. Today I stand stock still, an emotional chill leaving goosebumps in its wake. Instantly familiar, yet out of place in time, the warm sunlight sparkling on the dust I've stirred. I inhale the stale, amber atmosphere. My breath catches. For a moment the walls act strangely, arching towards the depth of my morning yawn. No. Making the sound of a dying seagull, "bhrugurhubrhu!" I shake the sleep away. Is that the sound a dying seagull makes? I've never been here. Where the hell am I even? Surreal. Where's the F-ing coffee?

I head into the kitchen, stepping over a pile of laundry some jerks left, as if the maid is going to hike in to wash it. Rooting through my pack I find a Ziplock of ground coffee, my Hello Kitty mug, and pour over filter. Getting some water going, I offer a silent prayer of thanks to the god of large white cylinders that are outdoor propane tanks. I lean against the counter and stare out the door while I wait.

Closing my eyes, I take another deep breath, trying to clear my head. How did I get here? Where am I? My backpack looks to be packed for days, and glancing at my legs, I'm pretty dirty. Few days at least. Maybe four?

The doorframe is covered in soot, as if there used to be a door that somehow was the only thing to burn. Fuck! I curse myself as I leap over to turn the stove off. There must have been a gas problem here! Wow, looks like I went to sleep, got just enough carbon monoxide poisoning to impair my short-term memory, when something ignited and blew the door out, dissipating the gas! I'm lucky to be alive!

I grab my pack and coffee gear, hustling outside. Snagging a cushion off the porch swing, I sit on the other side of the yard, near the tree line. After a moment's debate, I figure I'm far enough away and dig my pocket rocket stove out of my pack, getting the water going again.

∽৯৵

I've had two cups of coffee, breakfast, and I'm sitting over by the trees working on a third cup, staring blankly at the cabin. Everything is unpacked, strewn about in a semi-orderly fashion. Between the clothes, trash, and remaining food, it looks like I'm about halfway through a week-long backpacking trip. The last thing I remember is getting ready for a run, and that's vague at best, so clearly a significant memory gap.

Leaning back, I stare up at the trees, feeling sorry for myself. I don't have any maps. My phone is dead. I gave the cabin a quick once over for anything helpful, no dice. Who has a cabin in the woods without any maps or an emergency radio? How do I backpack out of here, being days into the trip, maybe 30 miles or more, and having no idea where I am or which way to go? I've never felt so alone, trapped, helpless.

I did find a bizarre picture on the bookshelf. Rachel, Ethan and I, plus some dude I don't know. The picture is impossible. I haven't seen either of them in years, and we look to be mid-twenties or so. Not to mention the last time the three of us laughed that way together... Well, early high school I guess. Photoshopped, but who the hell would do that and why is it here?

Bringing the photo out to my gear with me, I lean it against my empty backpack, facing me. It's beautiful really, an adult version of our little threesome, and the add-on guy looks like he fits right in. Rachel's standing on the edge of a cliff, throwing a full-bodied laugh at the cameraman. I'm next to her, all smiles doing some kind of dorky cheerleader-eske move, one arm up, the other on her back, my left leg straight up resting on Ethan's shoulder, who's next to me. The other guy is taller and has his arm around my foot and Ethan's neck, pretending to punch him in the stomach, and they're laughing hard.

Actually, beautiful isn't a good description of it. Bittersweet. Looking at it makes me want to smile and cry at the same time. What could I have done differently with my life, to have this camaraderie? This connection?

Ugh, I don't have time for this nonsense! Whatever reality someone was trying to show by creating this picture, that chance is long gone. It doesn't exist. Irritated, I fling it at the cabin.

Course I feel instantly guilty, flinching as it smacks a rock with a crack. Either Rachel or Ethan must have gone through a lot of trouble to make it, probably getting the picture of me from my mom. But this raises a barrage of questions! Am I back home? In the Blueridge somewhere? God, how much of my memory is missing? The only logical explanation for that picture involves one of them planting it. Meaning I don't remember flying home, telling mom my plans in enough detail for her to pass it on to Rachel or Ethan, and for one of them to beat me here. Convoluted. No way.

I go grab it, saddened to see the glass shattered. Carefully I remove the picture, collecting the glass into a pile on the ruined frame. Shaking the picture gently for any shards, a tiny piece of paper taped to the back starts to unfold! Excited, I tug it off completely.

> *If you gaze long enough into an abyss,*
> *the abyss will gaze back into you.*
> *- Friedrich Nietzsche.*

"Well that's fucking cryptic." I say aloud, frowning at the note.

I reread it several times, flip it over, nothing. It does sound like something Rachel would quote. Well, what's the abyss? What are you trying to say old friend?

Placing the picture back against my pack where it belongs, I prop the note in front of it, lean against a tree, and stare for a long moment. My eyes glaze, my mind wanders, and I remain one hundred percent epiphany-free. Instead, my head hurts.

Finally, I mutter, "Couldn't just write me a nice note, huh?" and leave that mystery alone, try to refocus on the problem at hand. Got to escape this abyss, then I'll worry about why one is looking at me.

There's a robin and a chipmunk that seem pretty friendly, kind of watching me from a few feet away, next to each other. Probably used to being fed.

"Do either of you know which way to go to find other humans? Do you have cousins in a nearby city perhaps? Maybe you've seen cars or a road? I'm in a bit of a bind."

They both cock their heads at me, the same direction, same angle, clearly listening, looking as much like twins as a chipmunk and robin can. It'd be cute if I didn't feel so stressed by the situation. As it stands, it's a bit creepy.

I tap myself on the nose a few times, "Suck it up, buttercup." Feels empty without the mirror though, and the one in the cabin was broken. I sigh.

Shaking it off, I jump up, do a little shadow box. "Ok Susan, this is silly. I am NOT helpless! It's just disconcerting coming into this situation with no context."

I roll my neck around, do a few jumping jacks. If I stretch my food out, I've got a week easy, probably more. There's running water in the cabin. The pile of laundry seems to indicate someone was here recently, so I could just hang out until someone turns up. Course if that picture is really from Rachel or Ethan, one of them will come looking for me here, eventually.

On the other hand, I don't like waiting around to be rescued. I must have followed a trail here. Be risky, but I could just hop on a trail and assume I'll get somewhere in a week of dedicated backpacking. What, a hundred miles in week? More? Surely I'd get somewhere. Water sources would be a risk, but it's pretty green here. Be even safer if I'm actually in the Blueridge, being much more inhabited than out West.

Putting my hands on my hips, I start adlibbing a little ditty, "Should I stay, then starve someday? Or leave this hood, die in the woods?"

Chuckling, I raise my arms and start gyrating about, but pause mid-air when no more lyrics surface. The question of how I should die arrested my epic rhymes it seems. Closing my eyes, I finish out the dance with some quiet humming and a few kicks.

Abruptly I shut it! Something is coming up the overgrown trail to the cabin. It's slow and noisy, bushwhacking along, got to be human. I tiptoe about ten steps away, down the tree line, ducking behind a large tree to watch.

A stately old man strolls into the yard, brushing leaves and twigs off his suit. He reaches up to adjust his bowtie, then smooths down his suit again, straightening his back to be rigidly erect, formal. Takes a few uncertain steps towards the cabin, then stops to pat his hair a little, dropping his arm to a right angle across his belly and just standing there, looking dignified.

After a moment his eyes find my pile of gear, studying it briefly, then follow the tree line until he spots me looking at him in astonishment, no longer trying to hide.

"Well Hello, Susan."

I'm not surprised to hear the slight English lilt. It's goddamn Batman's butler, Alfred.

2

Dumbfounded, I try to recover myself. "Uh, hi. You're that actor. Played Alfred in that dark Batman movie, the one with Batman's backstory. I'm sorry. I don't remember your name."

He looks down at his hands a moment, turning them over. "Am I? Did you see that movie recently?"

Irritated by the enigmatic response, but confused by his kindly stance and expression, I don't know what to say. Eventually I shrug, mumbling, "Um, no. When it first came out I guess."

He doesn't offer anything more, and starts looking around, taking in the yard and cabin, giving the impression I'm talking to a child who doesn't understand social cues.

I cover my eyes for a moment, and in exasperation, a little too aggressively, I shout, "Look, how do you know my name?"

He looks startled, lightly placing a hand on his chest. "Susan is our name. Of course I know it."

I glare at him.

He holds up both hands in a stop gesture. "Ok. I apologize. I am new to this. Let us speak plainly." Gesturing towards the cabin, "Can we sit on the porch swing? You have spent some time there, and it has looked lovely all along. This is a wonderful experience for me."

I try to check my anger. His intentions appear innocent, despite seeming increasingly crazy. I smile lightly, "Sounds nice, but the cabin is dangerous. Look at the doorframe."

He walks up to the cabin, examines the doorframe, rubbing some soot off and sniffing his fingers. Then disappears inside and I hear the water running.

After a moment, Alfred reappears in the doorway, gesturing for me to come over. I don't move. Feeling thoroughly disoriented, looking at this celebrity standing there, bizarrely dressed, speaking in riddles, acting like everything is normal, I feel like I need to wake up.

The notion hits me like a ton of bricks! I do need to wake up! There is no way this is real. I pinch myself a few times, build a welt on my forearm, which hurt way more than it should have. Didn't work, I'm still here.

Fine. I grab the cushion I was sitting on and walk back towards the cabin. Alfred smiles broadly.

I plop down on the swing, and he sits too, a polite distance away despite the small swing, his hands in his lap, staring forward. We rock gently, watching as the chipmunk and robin join us, climbing and flying, respectively, onto the railing.

Alfred continues to look around, taking it in, again giving off the vibe of a child, but this time in happy wonder. I eye him wearily.

Eventually he turns to me, "I do not believe the cabin is dangerous. I caused the soot somehow when I tried to stop you from leaving last time. Apparently it does not work that way. I cannot simply insert myself, but rather must enter in a plausible manner. I am surprised coming up the trail as Alfred is plausible, but I suppose it makes sense in context." He pauses a beat, then smiles broadly again, "I am very happy to be here."

Ok. Good? I don't know if I want to go further down this rabbit hole. Nothing he says makes sense. I close my eyes. It's a dream Susan. My subconscious is trying to tell me something. A riddle to decode.

Opening my eyes again, I see he's staring at me, "Exactly! Subconscious is how you would refer to me. I should have led with that. Hello, Susan. We are one. You, your conscious self, me, your subconscious!"

He looks out at the yard again, "Normally, I run the show a lot more than you realize, but my influence here has been minimal, and now we are here together somehow. We are in a bit of a bind, as you say."

Pieces start to click into place. Sure, the pieces are forming a most peculiar picture, but at least I understand what he's saying.

In a monotone I offer, "I've manifested my subconscious as Alfred, Batman's butler, in order to have a conversation."

He pats me on the knee, "I believe so, though it seems I had to force the issue."

I pinch myself again, "And I, er, 'we', are dreaming."

He frowns, furrows his brow, then leans back and swings a little, runs his hand along the armrest. "This is no dream. It is too concrete, and I am not in charge of it." He side-eyes me, looking abashed, "And…" He takes a deep breath, looks away. "And I am not functioning properly."

I stop the swing and turn towards him, pulling my right foot under my left leg so I can face him comfortably. "What do you mean, not functioning?"

Alfred scratches his neck uncomfortably, looking suddenly tearful, "I regulate all your base functions. I have done so well, like clockwork! For twenty-nine years!" He sighs. "Since we have been here, I have been unable to make you breathe properly. I cannot make sense of it. I am very sorry. I have been trying."

Leaning forward he rests his head in his hands. I have the need to comfort him, but feel embarrassed about it, like trying to console my grandfather about his failing health. Our failing health! I reach over and rub his back.

He turns towards me again, mirroring the way I'm sitting, which looks awkward for an old man. Taking my hands, eyes wet, he straightens up, and I can imagine him thinking, 'Suck it up, buttercup.' Actually, I notice with a start, he did think it!

He smiles lightly, giving my hands a squeeze, looking a little hopeful. "I lost control of your heart rhythm earlier, but got it back!" A glint of triumph in his eyes that fades as fast as it arose. "Even so, we need to breathe."

Dropping my hands, he looks out at the yard.

"I expect we are dying."

3

We rock in silence for a moment. I am absolutely overwhelmed. Floored. I count ten slow breaths, trying to calm, refocus. Finally, I decide one thing at a time. I need information. My subconscious here seems to know more than I do.

Rubbing his back again, "It's ok Alfred. Can I call you Alfred?"

He shrugs, offers that same gentle smile.

"You said you can't make me breathe 'properly'. So I am breathing?"

He nods, "I believe so, but abnormally. I cannot get us back on track."

"And my heart is beating?"

He beams a little, "Oh yes! I can feel it. Da-dum, Da-dum, Da-dum. Just like it is supposed to!"

Ok. "So we are not dead then. What happened when you lost control of my heart rhythm?"

Sensitive topic. Looking ashamed, he shrugs again, "I could not understand it. The signal between chambers became slow and erratic, sluggish, and your heartbeat grew quite slow. It was very scary. I gave up on the upper chambers, made the lower beat as fast as I could, but then it was too fast." Squinting, as if trying to examine the trees across the yard, "I got it back though! Da-dum, da-dum, da-dum!"

I must have had a cardiac arrythmia. With a shudder I imagine I'm lying face down in a stream somewhere, 'breathing abnormally' as the current occasionally bobs my mouth above water. That doesn't sound survivable, but if I do make it, maybe I should stop running alone up in the mountains all the time.

"What was I doing before that happened?"

He peers at me. "Sounds like you already know, running."

Standing up, I begin pacing in front of Alfred and the swing. "You said you tried to stop me from leaving 'last time'. What did you mean?"

Looking suddenly buoyed, he jumps up next to me, stopping my pacing with his hands on my shoulders, "It has been amazing! You have been reliving this cabin scene with different people. It was so wonderful to see Rachel and Ethan again! I have missed them so!"

Stunned, I blink for a moment, trying to process! As the enormity of the situation hits me, I suppress a sob. I am lying somewhere dying and my brain builds this elaborate scenario in order to bring Rachel and Ethan in for a happy reunion? The more I think about it, the more the sob threatens to escape! I spend a few moments waffling. Sniffle, swallow, choke, sniffle, hard swallow, choke, shaking out my hands, losing it but desperately trying to stay focused on saving my life!

It's no use. Oh Rachel! Ethan! I'm dying! This is too much all at once! Devastated, moaning, I throw myself back onto the swing and begin to cry. Not my usual, stoic, expressionless stare with tears leaking out, but an outright snotty, whimpering, shuddering, full bodied bawl. It's an epic cry of the sort I've not had since I crushed Jasper's motorcycle. Alfred pats me awkwardly on the back, as I had been for him, and I snot all over my sleeve. Increasingly it feels cathartic.

After only a few minutes it's out of my system. I feel calm and more whole than I have in years. I AM going to save my life! Not just for me, but to reconnect with my friends. I've been such a fool.

Alfred smiles down at me, "That was your fourth time. I think you needed it."

Looking up at him, I am so grateful he is here, "Thank you, Alfred, for finding your way here to join me. Let's figure this out."

He offers a modestly satisfied look for a moment, but then gets serious, taking his turn to do the pacing. "Every time you fell, I thought, well this is it. The end! We keep restarting here, but how many times will this happen? Is this an indefinite loop? What does it even mean for me to 'feel' our heartbeat here? Are we dead already and this is the last spurt of us, of energy escaping our body, cycling in the ether? Are we simply creating happy times with our dearest friends until our body runs out of oxygen?"

He shakes his hands in front of him, as though flinging something dirty off them. "I do not understand the rules in this place, but a calming happy reunion to ease the pain of death seems the most likely. Here we are, standing in our tunnel, walking towards the light. The last time you started to leave, I became convinced I needed to intervene somehow, but I could not make it through! Gram was even here briefly, trying to take you away!"

He stomps his foot, making a fist and shaking it at the trees. "We are too young to die!"

I'm a little taken aback by Alfred's passion, but it feeds a blossom of warmth and hope inside me. I let out a big breath, deflating like a balloon, accepting that his last interpretation is probably the most likely. Occam's razor. Gram was here? Jesus. An uphill battle for us.

"I've been falling?"

He sits next to me again. "Yes, a cliff. To our death. It is horrifying and excruciating every time. I am glad you do not remember it."

We rock for a while, each lost in our own thoughts. I am emotionally exhausted trying to accept and process this reality, and don't know what to do about it. As I mentally replay our conversation, I pause on his comment that it was my fourth bawl.

Bopping him on the arm for not thinking to volunteer the info, "Who else has been here with me?"

He smiles broadly again, almost channeling Ethan's goofy smile, and leans back, putting his arm behind me on the back of the swing. "Well, Rachel and Ethan were here separately. John was the first iteration."

Frowning, I lean against his side so his arm's around me, again feeling as though I'm with my grandfather, but more comfortably than earlier, "Who's John?"

Alfred barks a laugh, "I was very proud to see John here. I sent many signals that he was a suitable mate! He was like Oliver in that way. I am responsible for processing smell. You often don't seem to care, but I always release a mess of hormones when I detect the most appropriate pheromones!"

I shudder. If this John is anything like Oliver, he is obviously a terrible mate.

Sensing my thought, "That is not fair. You and I see it differently. He was an exceptional match with our DNA, thus you would have had very healthy offspring and successfully passed on our genes. You liked John aside from my signals though. He might have been both a good mate and a good match."

He smiles proudly, straightening his bowtie with his free hand, "Actually, smell and pheromones have been a theme of each iteration, my primary contribution to this place! At least until I forced my way into it physically."

I shrug. We're talking about a stranger. "Hold on a sec. How can you remember John when I don't?"

Alfred laughs again, and shakes a finger at me. "Some part of you remembers him. I did not bring him here! You saturated the both of us with alcohol the night we met him. He had to carry you up the stairs of our apartment, and left a sticky note for you to call him."

He pokes me in the side with his finger, saying a little bitterly, "I released the hormones when you saw the note too, a small breach of etiquette without his pheromones present, but you still did not care."

This is vaguely familiar. Back in college, I did wake up to a sticky note asking me out once, after a blackout night of too much partying. Not remembering how I got home, I was just grateful to be fully clothed! Learned my lesson, scaling way back on the drinking after that. Looking back at it, I think I did masturbate a few times that morning, notable as it was so unusual with a brutal hangover.

"Whatever. None of this matters. What do we do now Alfred?"

His smile fades. He scratches his neck. Briefly we make eye contact, and then decisively lean forward, placing our hands on the swing to get up, but then we stop, all in unison. We lean back again, staring out at the yard.

What do we do now?

4

We sat and rocked for a long time.

Alfred walked me through parts of the other iterations, a simultaneously fascinating, magical, and heartbreaking exercise. We looked for clues and answers in the little details, but didn't have any epiphanies. He's just as confused as I am on the bizarre Nietzsche quote, though we decided the cabin itself could be an abyss of some kind.

We tried to identify the points in our life where each iteration diverged from the reality I know, which seems to boil down to John's sticky note and Rachel's butterfly handjob (Ha! Holy shit!). And we had a lengthy debate over the validity of the content in the prior iterations, which got heated after discussing Rachel's fractal and multiverse nonsense.

The other iterations are easy for me to dismiss, not remembering them, but Alfred insists they were real. He believes some part of Rachel was actually here, and some part of *that* part of Rachel, her Alfred maybe, understood what was going on, inspiring the multiverse discussion in the first place.

This all made my head hurt, and I dismissed it as pure rubbish until he pointed out, if the prior iterations weren't real, then this one isn't either. That's a bit of a mindfuck, since I'm sitting here living it.

He also got miffed when I argued he was far too sentient for a brainstem, but forgot all about it when I made him a PB&J, absorbed in the experience of eating instead of his usual vicarious enjoyment while I eat.

All in all, just your average day hanging out in fantasy land with Batman's butler, the grandfatherly manifestation of your subconscious mind.

In truth, it's been some of the most relaxed, comfortable, easiest, fuck it the best, companionship I've had in some time. And no, the irony is not lost on me, since I suppose I'm actually just talking to myself.

∽∾

Searching for any little plan to grasp, something inconsistent hits me, "Alfred, you said each iteration starts the same way, just like today, my coming to, standing in the living room awash in the feeling I've been there before?"

He nods, eyebrows raised, waiting for my point.

I sit up straight in the swing, "Well, why did the first iteration start that way? *Have* I been here before?"

Looking disappointed, he shrugs, "We have dreamed of a cabin in the mountains for years, fulfilled by that little house you bought in Montana."

Frustrated, I slouch back in the swing. This explanation seems incomplete though, and whining a little, I push the thought, "But I feel like I was here as a child, I don't remember wanting a cabin until I was older!"

Rubbing his temples, "Hm. You were fairly young. I first spun a dream of a cabin in your early teens." He pauses a beat,

"You know, I believe it was simply a realistic and attainable manifestation of the castle you daydreamed after Jasper broke your heart. I have never thought of it that way, but it seems obvious with both fresh in my mind."

I don't like the idea of Jasper having any influence over me, and I cringe as Alfred casually states he broke my heart. Sighing, I realize it's the truth. That's exactly what happened.

I shake it off. This has got to mean something! "So I'm dying, and wham, my brain brings me here! Why?" I stare at Alfred a second, then pop up, heading into the cabin. "Come on!"

I stand stock still in the living room. Closing my eyes, I try to recapture the feeling from this morning. Alfred stands in the doorway, attentive. Quietly, I think it through out loud, "That was clearly a pivotal moment in my life. Everyone talks about my childhood like it was so idyllic because of Rachel and Ethan, and I always dismiss it. I don't remember it that way. I remember being isolated, rejected. Alone. But you know what? It was idyllic! I threw it away. It was me, not Jasper! I chose to be alone!"

Putting my hands on my head, I open my eyes and stare at Alfred. "Sure, he was the catalyst. He derailed my childhood spectacularly! But I didn't have to wallow in it for the last nineteen years! Christ!"

I'm pacing the room now, gesticulating at the walls, spilling out angry energy. "I chose to focus on the negative. I chose not to lean on my friends. I refused to accept their love. I wouldn't allow myself to love them, to be vulnerable! I threw myself into meaningless relationships because I didn't have to care. They were safe! I moved thousands of miles away. I bought an isolated home. I became a goddamn recluse. I, I, I!"

I pause, huff, throw my hands in the air. "Me!"

I'm in the middle of the room, breathing a little too hard, arms now hanging limp at my sides. Alfred's still in the doorway, standing very straight in his suit, looking like he wants to get me tea or something.

After a moment he smiles, "Yes, we cannot change what happens to us, but we can do our best to choose how we react."

I smile back. "Alfred, what runs through our mind at the start of each iteration? Something about magic and mystery?"

Knowing exactly what I'm asking he recites, "A treasure waiting in every closet, behind every book, under a secret floorboard."

We blink at each other briefly, then I start tearing books off the shelves. Nothing. I'm about to decide that was dumb when I notice one of the little paperbacks, looking awkward the way it fell to the floor. Something about the way it's laying. It should have fallen open, be bent with the heavy hardback leaning on it. Instead it's firmly closed, and supporting the heavier book despite the angle.

I pick it up and something rattles inside. It's *The Catcher in the Rye*, my favorite when I was a teenager, but of course it's not actually a book. There's a little clasp. Flipping it open, sure enough, the ornate iron key I melted in the castle fireplace. Eyes wide, I press the cool metal to my cheek.

Alfred's one step ahead of me, already on his knees rummaging through boxes in the closet when I catch up. It's dark in there, but it doesn't matter. With childlike excitement he lets out a 'Whoop' and stands up, cradling something.

Setting it on the bed so we can see it in the light from the window, a dusty treasure chest, about the size of a shoebox. We might as well be pirates.

The key slides in easily. Inside, a toy model car. A pale blue International Harvester Scout II. I have no doubt it's the 1978 model. Picking it up, the passenger side door falls open, making me laugh. I place it on the floor, next to the wall. Stare at it a moment.

I look up at Alfred, and he nods once. Together we start making the rumbling engine noises, and then I try to hum with the wavering voice that engine always gave me. Gingerly I push the Scout into the wall with my foot and we move into dramatic metal on metal noises! Alfred throws himself to the floor, imitating a tinkling, rattling sound and then lays still, both feet and arms in the air, as if the motorcycle was actually a dead rat.

Tears stream down my cheeks, part laughter, part heartbreak, part release! I pull him up next to me, into a big bear hug. We're both laugh crying.

Getting ahold of myself, I take a step back and shake my head, mumbling, "Jesus Christ Jasper, I was ten."

Suddenly I grab hold of Alfred's arm and point emphatically at the Scout. "This! This is the butterfly effect! One moment changed my whole fucking life! But I am done with that now. I am making my own choices now. I choose my friends! I choose life, and love, and connection! I am not afraid to be vulnerable!" I kick it across the floor. "I am not afraid."

Alfred's eyes crinkle with pride. "Me neither. Where is the secret floorboard?"

I go to my knees right where I'd put the Scout, run my hands over the floor. Right against the wall, a tiny hook allowing me to lift about six inches of the floorboard. Underneath, an envelope covered in dust.

I sit back against the bedframe, staring at the envelope. I pat the floor beside me and Alfred sits too.

Blowing out a big breath, I wiggle my finger in and tear it open. A single sheet of paper, blank except for the very bottom, where it says 'I love you both, I always have, I always will.'

I hold it to my chest for a long moment, and then hand it to Alfred. "Is this the end of Rachel's suicide note?"

He looks at it for a second, and slowly shakes his head. Turning towards me, his eyes wet but aglow, "No Susan. That is our handwriting."

5

Taking the letter back, slowly I fold it up, making the creases with extra care, and slip it into my pocket.

I pull my knees up against my chest and rest my chin against them. "Alfred, we've been looking for answers here, and I think we found them." Hugging my legs tightly, self-soothing, I sigh, "But that's not the answer we're looking for. Is the purpose of this place really just to show me the importance of Rachel and Ethan as I'm dying? How do we save ourselves?"

Alfred idly pulls my shoelace, then flicks it with a finger. "I do not know. Perhaps you can hike out, knowing the chipmunk and robin will try to stop you?"

This doesn't feel right. I lean my forehead on a knee, mumbling to my chest, "What, you think I'll get to the other side of the cliff, walk through a magic door, and suddenly find I'm lying in a stream, barely breathing? Stand up out of the stream, walk out?"

He looks over at me. Looks back down, picks up my shoelace again, shrugs.

Standing, I put my hand on the wall, push it a bit. "Alfred, I need to wake up."

He stands too, listlessly. "We are not dreaming Susan."

I punch the wall. Hurts my knuckles, too real. Makes my forearm ache sharply, from the previous falls I suppose. The iterations clearly bleed into each other.

Rubbing my arm, "You said my forearm hurt in the first iteration. I've fallen Alfred. I was running, I fell, but survived. The stream I'm in is at the bottom of a ravine. Do I need to intentionally throw myself off the cliff? Wake up in the stream?"

Pursing his lips at me, clearly in thought. "That cliff is not survivable, it is thousands of feet. The pain of impact is sudden and agonizing, but then instantly we are in the cabin living room again. What would you do differently?"

I shrug, exasperated. "I don't know! Focus on waking up for real? Sheer determination not to come back here?"

He's staring. "I am afraid we would not wake up at all, but I am willing to try. My presence here could be anchoring you. We will jump together."

Putting his hands behind his head, he blows out a breath. "If we do 'wake up for real' as you say, I believe we would wake up into not breathing properly, suffocating. We are here as a comfort, so we do not have to experience that pain."

I set my jaw, standing up straighter. "I am not going to die without a fight."

Alfred squints lightly at me, nods once. "What is the plan?"

I start to head out into the yard to gather my gear, trying to organize my thoughts, but pause at the gaping, soot covered doorframe.

"Alfred? How did you burn this door down?"

He stops behind me, smiles, "Well, sheer determination is a good way to look at it. I was not going to let you leave and

I balled up all my energy and focus as tightly as possible, releasing it all at once with everything I had! Forced my way here. Actually, I got the idea from you, when you broke the bathroom mirror and left those handprints."

Getting excited, "Alfred! Can you do that again? From inside to get out?"

His eyes light up. "I do not know. But that is much better than flinging ourselves off the cliff!"

I slap the counter, kick one of the cabinets, flex at the clock on the wall. "I'll do it too! We'll either wake up or tear this place to pieces!"

Calming, I put my hand on Alfred's chest. "I suppose I won't remember this, but you might. Can you signal me in some way?"

That gentle smile slides into place, "I send many signals. What do you want me to say?"

I bite my lip, "I will be afraid to contact Rachel and Ethan. Signal me to do it anyway."

He nods solemnly. "It is a breach of etiquette, but I will send extra oxytocin whenever you think of them. It is the hormone responsible for bonding and connection. Once you reconnect, I will have to resume normal levels."

I grab the letter and slip it into Alfred's shirt pocket, patting his chest lightly, "You have my permission. Thank you, Alfred. For everything."

Resting his hand on top of mine, he straightens up a little taller. "My friend, it has always been an honor, for twenty-nine years."

Squeezing my hand once, he walks into the living room, taking his suit coat off for the first time and folding it carefully, laying it on the couch. He flexes a little, rolls his neck around, then squats slightly, bunching up his shoulders. He looks incredibly tense.

The chipmunk runs in, striding upright, showing me his grizzly bear routine for the first time! He's chittering and running around at Alfred's feet, throwing his nut, running to get it, throwing it again. The robin is flying circles around the living room, peeping away! They look more excited than mad though, and I feel a wave of heat coming from the room.

Suddenly Alfred stands up straight, flinging his arms out, bright light bleeding from his fingers! The chipmunk stops, imitating his stance, head back, tiny beads of light on his claws! The robin too, now on Alfred's shoulder, wing tips aglow.

I'd been watching, mouth agape, squinting against the growing light, and I shake it off. I didn't realize it would happen so fast! I sprint to the bathroom!

Slipping my hands into the handprints, snug as gloves, I bunch up my shoulder muscles, grip as hard as I can, tense my back and legs, every muscle I can! I look up into the shattered mirror.

The Susan Picasso stares back, but only for a moment. The multifaceted picture begins to morph and bend, a corner of my shirt bleeding into a hazy image of Ethan, goofy smile and all, an ear melting into Rachel, laughing boisterously. From their separate spots in the mirror, but in unison, they each straighten and hold a single hand up, a solemn greeting, or perhaps a farewell. Before I can decide, I'm distracted by a stray hair splitting into tree branches, then blossoming into the shady oak!

Dominating the mirror, at the very center, the cracks begin to reverse, joining, and several broken pieces of my face slide into each other, liquifying, merging, a jagged piece of my chin, a nostril, an eye, an eyebrow, an amalgamation of Susan pieces drooping and smearing! Something else entirely takes shape!

A ravine, a narrow and rocky crevice at the bottom of a short drop, maybe thirty feet.

Yes! With a scream I leap and try to tear the sink out of the counter, slamming my head into the mirror!

Abruptly black. The void.

PART V

Death seems so final.
Nothingness seems so very, very irrevocable and permanent.
But then, if it is,
what about the nothingness that was before you started?

"Inevitable Ecstasy", Session Four, Alan Watts

1

Hello?
Rachel?
Mom? Mother?
Wha-? Where? Who? Who's there?
Hello? HELLO!? It's me, Suzy. I, I am scared. Hello?
Silence. Deafening. Panicking, I scream! The racket echoes through my mind, but I don't think I made a sound.
I try to calm, focus, listen.
A rush. Air?
I float.
I am lost.
RACHEL?!

2

Breathe.

I glance about to find… What? My eyes are open, but it's so dark. A liquid black, an infinite absorption. I blink and blink, squint into nothing. Distantly, I sense Rachel. She's desperately speaking to me. Muted. It seems odd I can't hear her, but I can't find a reason to worry. She's here. I am remarkably comfortable, and a profound sense of peace suddenly swallows my fear. I smile lightly, exhale a long, slow breath, and accept the nothing.

Floating, I relax, focus. I wave my arms and legs, no sensation. Closing my eyes, I listen again, but sound closes off around me, like the cabin of an airplane pressurizing, a sensation of forced silence, of isolation. Something's there? Just out of reach. Yes, a feeling of something lost, but present. A favorite song flittering in the sub-conscious recesses I can't quite access. My long dead grandmother's face not quite remembered. It's there, but lost in time. Something my subconscious knows, keeping trapped below sea level.

"I am here." A soft English lilt, not a voice I recognize, but instantly familiar, comforting, as though Ethan grew old in England.

"Hello? Where am I? What's happening? I cannot see."

"I see you. I do not know. Perhaps we have died."

"I... What?"

3

Breathe.

I glance about to find myself in an oddly familiar room, a doorknob in hand. I cannot feel my forearm below the elbow, and I fumble at the door. This moment's distraction opens another door. Awoken behind me, she sends a love letter, stamped, earnestly mailed, strawberry perfumed with the taste of her lips, complete with understanding, compassion and a plea, backed by ten years growing up together. All at once I'm overwhelmed with every laugh, every smile, the years culminating into something more than connection, her confusing desires as we move into puberty, the way she looks at me as we whisper about boys, eventually love, LOVE, feelings blossoming unchecked throughout our inseparable and ideal friendship. She rolls it all into a neat little package as she breathes my name.

"Suzy."

I pause at the door, stunned, doorknob in hand. A moment of decision frozen in time. Slowly, gently, time collapses on itself. I turn.

Her expression's a little sorrowful, but so full of love I catch my breath. No expectation, only acceptance. Of me. Of everything that is Susan. Tinged with loss, but not sadness. Something expansive shining in her eyes that swallows up any sorrow, fear, vulnerability. Something that aches, but only because it longs to be shared and it's too big to ever fully do so. Something… Perfect.

Oh! Oh Rachel! "Rachel, I'm sorry." I take a deep breath. "I'm sorry I can't love you the way you love me. I miss you." Eyes wet now, softer, "I'm sorry I wasn't there when you needed me. I…"

We stare at each other. Standing up a little straighter, I whisper, "I love you."

Her expression sits a moment, frozen, then gently slides into her half smile. Slowly, almost imperceptibly, she nods. Sitting up on an arm, she reaches her other hand out to me.

Suddenly inundated with a surge of relief, of… joy, my breath catches. I close my eyes as the feeling washes over me in a wave and I feel whole. Inhaling fast and deep, I strain my lungs to capacity, memory and oxygen both suffusing me with life, desperately, as though I've clawed to the surface half drowned. Smiling, feeling light, I hold it in for a few seconds, relish it. Opening my eyes, I return to reality, stare at my best friend on the couch before me.

Indescribable. I take a step towards her, but the world tilts impossibly, tossing me to the floor.

No, not the floor. The ground, the field, the oak. For a moment I savor the smell of the nearby grass, listen to the birds tweet and flutter about up in the branches. The sunlight flickers through the leaves.

A sob behind me, anguish! Disoriented, I roll over.

I am fifteen. Ethan's a mess, bawling, apologizing like a madman, completely losing control. A part of me is dying to take it all back, enfold him into my arms and beg for forgiveness right then, comfort him. But I can't. I just can't! Standing, I turn to leave him there.

I nearly smack into Rachel. Impossible! She's old! An adult!

I'm squinting at this vision of twenty-something Rachel, trying to process her bizarre appearance, right as she slaps me. Hard, knocking me back to the ground. I steady myself with a hand on a root, the other gently touching my cheek, aflame. I look up at her, my eyes wild, afraid.

She rubs the palm of her hand on her shirt, no doubt on fire as well. Remarkably, her eyes become kind, and the half smile drifts into place.

Nodding once, she leans over and pokes me in the side, "Ok. That's done. You deserved that. I hope it bruises." And walks over to Ethan.

Confused, I turn towards a truly anachronistic scene. Rachel and Ethan are nearly the same height, and I can't fight the sensation she's standing on a stool.

He's befuddled too. Rubbing his eyes aggressively, he blinks her way, then stares at her chest a moment, making her laugh hardily. Ethan and I involuntarily chuckle.

Reaching over, she wipes a few of his tears away, then makes a show of wiping the snot from his nose with the back of her hand. He smiles between sniffles as she takes him into her arms.

Ethan stares at me over her shoulder, eyes red and puffy. He looks sad, but not angry. After a moment he lifts a hand my way in a kind of salute, and offers a rare closed mouth smile.

I cannot understand and I try to process, to rationalize what's happened, certain an adult Rachel is not actually here. Suddenly I find the scene blurred, and a wave shudders the oak, almost seaweed swaying underwater. The powerful mirage sends a small chill head to toe, dizzying, and I squinch my eyes shut tightly to stop the dancing tree.

Opening them again I find the tree, the field, gone! My daddy stands in the doorway. His eyes harden and he suddenly takes an aggressive step into my room, jabbing a finger towards me, inadvertently flinging a speck of blood onto the wall. I cower, sniveling, making myself as small as possible in the corner, the crack of flesh on flesh still reverberating through my brain. I am blind with the terror of my own beating I am sure has arrived!

No! No! NO! That. Is. It! Somehow the wheel is turning backwards but I am getting off. I bunch up my shoulder muscles, grip the handle of my dresser as hard as I can, tense my back and legs, every muscle I can!

I look up into my father's eyes. No.

I blink. I am, what, twenty-nine? Yes. I live in Montana where I own a tiny home. I nod once, and glance about. Yet here I stand, a ghost lost in my childhood bedroom, stuck in a memory, frozen in time.

I look over at Jasper, and shake my head. Unbelievable. He looks so different through my adult eyes, no longer the angry behemoth from my childhood memory. He is insecure, scared, god, maybe even heartbroken. I think I see it. Something more than that damn motorcycle.

Well he was twenty-two when I was born, so I guess he's thirty-two here, barely older than I am now. I sure haven't figured things out. Still, I mean Jesus Christ I was ten. Some things you just do not do. Taking him in, I frown, shake my head at him again. Bastard.

I turn to my ten-year-old self, cowering on the floor, terrified. Now that is heartbreaking. Crouching down I take her hand, and she slowly comes to life, looking up at me, eyes wide in wonder. I can feel she accepts this as a daydream, a fantasy, simply one more of the many.

Grasping for something profound to say, I whisper, "Suzy, this is not your fault. There are emotions at play so much bigger than us."

Not sure what to make of this declaration, she doesn't respond, looking down at my hand. I squeeze hers, and her eyes spring back up to mine, leaking tears on both sides.

Being here reminds me of the fantasy she's about to have, locking her heart up in a castle. I contemplate telling her to forget it, to walk right up to Rachel and Ethan, cry it out with them instead. But that's too much to ask. This was too devastating, and demands a deep, emotionally powerful response from within. She needs that castle to seal off the bleed, prop up her soul with internal strength.

"Suzy, make spare keys. Leave two extras on a pedestal outside the castle." I close my eyes picturing how this will work, "Yes, put them in two ornate wooden lockboxes, each with a code. Rachel's birthday and Ethan's birthday. No one else can open them, but our friends will know what to do."

She furrows her eyebrows at me, shrugs. I suppose she'll understand what I mean in a few minutes. I don't know what else to say.

Sighing, I take her in my arms and she begins to whimper, shaking quietly. I hold her for a long time, afraid the scene will resume if I let go.

Eventually she calms, becoming still, her head resting against me. Another long moment, and I pull away to take her in once more.

There's something I was desperate to do when I was here nineteen years ago. "I'm going to check on mom, but I'll be back in a second to go through this with you."

She nods, watching me silently.

I duck under Jasper's outstretched arm and press myself flat against the doorjamb as I slip by, careful not to touch him, afraid to wake the beast.

The living room is not exactly here, unfortunately. Mom's legs, motionless amongst the detritus of the broken bowl, are swallowed by a wall of color. I'm blocked from actually checking on her by a smeared, impressionistic version of the room, painted at the point beyond where my ten-year-old self could see. It's beautiful really, as though Monet stood just out of sight, whimsically encapsulating the memory.

I touch the wall, causing a light shimmer, and press my hand through. It vanishes from sight, the wall unchanged beyond a ripple now encircling my arm. It's warm, maybe damp? I can't touch anything.

I stare a moment, frowning lightly, then press my face to the Monet to look.

4

A flash! And suddenly I'm overwhelmed with the sensation of movement, fast, as though I'm hurtling headfirst down a frictionless tunnel. More flashes follow, each accompanied by a brief pause before I plunge down another tunnel.

Abruptly I'm sitting on a swing, rocking lightly, pushing my toes into the dirt. Rachel holds the chain from behind, absently swaying with me. We are seven.

A boy strides up with his hands cupped together, his toothy smile absorbs his face.

"Hey! Want to see something amazing?"

I turn to Rachel, who offers a half smile. Unspoken assent passes between us and we lean in to peer at his hands.

He opens them ever so slightly and instantly a tiny, terrified frog leaps out onto my face! I scream, falling backwards out of the swing onto Rachel, who grunts in surprise. My right shoelace catches in the swing's chain, snaring my foot, and we struggle in a heap in the dirt, a misshapen turtle stuck on its back. The boy looks abashed, hastily fumbling with the chain to free my shoelace.

I'm angry, jumping up to yell at the boy, when Rachel's boisterous laugh from the ground stops me. Looking down at her, the boy and I both start chuckling gently.

Smiling up at us, she jibes the boy, "You're right, that was amazing."

He nods appreciatively, flashing that toothy smile, but it quickly slides into furrowed brows and concern, "But you let Goliath get away!"

Rachel frowns, her eyebrows set with determination, and pops onto her knees in the dirt. "Not for long! Let's go!"

Immediately the three of us begin carefully crawling through the dirt into the grass, searching intently for the tiny escapee.

A wave of sadness passes through me, and I look up from the grass to realize I'm no longer in the playground, but rather alone in my front yard. Somehow I'm smaller, younger.

A ball of emotions explodes! Alice got some stupid A on some stupid thing last week and Daddy was so proud, putting it right on the fridge, but I drew the most best dragon today and he didn't care! I gave it to him twice! It belongs on the fridge! It's not fair! The tears well up, out of control. I collapse into the grass and weep.

After a few minutes I realize a little girl has sat next to me, her bike abandoned on the sidewalk. She's staring quietly out at the street.

Mystified, I look up at her. She glances down, offers half a smile, then looks back out at the street. I'm not sure what to make of her silence, but I've forgotten my tears and sit up beside her, trying to determine what she's looking at.

We sit this way for a long moment. I don't think she's looking at anything.

Suddenly she pops up and strolls over to the Magnolia, starts to climb. Three branches up she leans out towards me, dramatically flinging out her free arm. "Aren't you coming?"

Smiling, I run over, determined to catch her despite the multi-branch lead! She giggles and climbs faster.

Grabbing the lowest branch I'm startled to realize I'm holding the doorjamb in the living room, my brand-new stuffed raccoon clutched tightly at my side. It's late and I am scared.

I see the source of the noise that woke me. Daddy is leaning over the couch scowling, wiping up a mess on the side table, a brown bottle in hand.

He upends the bottle for whatever's left and heads into the kitchen, stumbling lightly on the rug. The hall's dark behind me and I stand unnoticed, watching as he grabs another bottle from the fridge. He plops back onto the couch with a sigh, picking up an orange pill bottle from the floor.

Now I know we're not supposed to play with those orange bottles! I shuffle over to him, gently stepping over several crumpled balls of paper, and put my little hand on top of his.

"Daddy, no." I whisper.

Surprised by my appearance, he smiles lightly, though it doesn't reach his eyes. Slowly he places the orange bottle on the side table, leans back into the couch, takes a long swig of his drink. Stares at me.

He looks really sad, so I hand him Raccoon. He smiles lightly again, this time his eyes twitching, growing a little wet. I've never seen Daddy this way, but I know I'm helping. I place my hand on his knee and pat it.

Slouching on the couch, Daddy holds my best friend in both hands, at arm's length down between his knees, staring at him.

Finally he sighs and carefully snuggles Raccoon against his side, pats him for a second. He looks around, pulls the throw blanket from the couch and wraps the edge around Raccoon's torso, tucking him in. Something inside me blooms gently. I beam at Daddy.

"There." He says, patting him again, smoothing the blanket.

Slowly he looks back at me, his eyebrows bunching together worriedly. He slurs, "It'sa late Suzy. What are you doing up?"

The sour smell of his Daddy drink wafting into my face erodes my smile. I wince and wrinkle my nose, stepping back.

He chuckles lightly, waving a hand in front of his face. "Sorry about that. Guess I woke you up. Sorry about that too." Then he frowns, staring past me. "I'm sorry about a lot of things."

Looking back at me, he stares in silence. I keep patting his knee.

He lets out a tremendous sigh, deflating like a balloon, and shakes his head. "You look so much like your daddy."

My heart skips a beat! Far and away the best compliment he's ever given me! Immediately I crawl into his lap and wrap my arms around his neck. Hesitantly he wraps his around me too.

I rest my head on his shoulder and relish the feeling, every part of my little body vibrating! A pure joy, an unbridled exuberance threatens to escape and I force myself still, afraid to break the embrace. Suddenly I'm shocked and a bit terrified to realize he's crying! I hold on tight.

"I miss him Suzy."

I don't know what to make of this. "Miss who Daddy?" I whisper.

He was rubbing my back, and freezes abruptly. After a moment he picks me up and places me back on the floor, ruffles my hair a little. We're back to staring.

"You're such a brave little girl. You take care of your mother and sister ok?" He grabs Raccoon and hands him back to me. "Here, Raccoon will always be there to help."

I nod. He pats me on the bottom, pushing me back towards the door. Message received, I slowly walk towards my room. Glancing back from the doorway, I see he's got the orange pill bottle in his hand again. Seeing me watching, he puts it back down, pats it once, sighs. I walk into the dark hallway.

It's darker than I thought, but with an eerie reddish glow. Actually, I can't really see anything, and I don't have Raccoon anymore. I'm floating gently. There are muffled sounds. Voices I think, but I can't understand. It's peaceful, and I float.

The noises turn staccato, angry. I feel increasingly anxious. After a few moments I bunch up my shoulder muscles, grip my little fists as hard as I can, tense my back and legs, every muscle I can! I want to cry, but instead I blink and come to. Right. I am twenty-nine.

I still can't see anything beyond this reddish glow about me, but now the muffled gibberish makes sense, forming words.

"… do you mean, more than five months? I was deployed before that."

Silence. A sigh. "Jasp."

"It's not mine. It's not MINE?! What the fuck Marie?"

"I didn't have to tell you. You'd have believed premature."

"How fucking noble! You… You cheated on me! What the FUCK? What. The. FUCK?! How could you?!"

"A mistake. God it was such a terrible mistake Jasper! I was so lonely. He was so helpful with Alice." A big gulp. "Look I'm not going to make excuses. There are no excuses. It was one goddamn horrible mistake!! I love you."

"Don't say that!!"

Silence. Heavy breathing. I'm shifted a little. I think mom stood up.

"Look. I want you to…"

Interrupting. "Who?"

"Jasper."

"WHO?"

Mom whispers, and I have to strain to make out the muffled sound. "Rick."

Silence again. Then Jasper merely replies, "Rick." Stunned. Somehow he doesn't sound angry anymore.

I'm jostled a little, and I picture Jasper taking Mom's shoulders, or maybe she's trying to hug him. Both?

"Is this…" He falters, recovering with a light breath, "Is this related to the accident?"

Mom lets out a light moan. Then begins to spill out a diatribe, "Jasper, I told him I was pregnant and we got into this huge fight. He wanted me to leave you. Said we'd been friends forever and this was always meant to be. Alice should have been his. Loved me for as long as he could remember. Oh how did he say it exactly? 'As a point in fact, I have no memory of not loving you.' Or something. It was sweet and awful all at the same time! I asked him how he could possibly ask me to leave you and he said you'd understand, that you were his best friend, that you could be a part of our family to the extent you wanted, but that I belonged with him."

I can feel Mom's heart beating fast.

Jasper, still stunned, "Rick."

"Well I told him in no uncertain terms I had made a horrible mistake and would never leave you. That he was a horrible person for suggesting it. He glared for the briefest of moments, nodded slowly, then left. I was shaken, but thought he would be ok. I'm sure he drove up to the Blue Ridge to blow off some steam, to think. Ran off the road, the deer…"

Quietly she whispers, "You know the rest."

"Rick."

I'm jostled again as Mom sighs, exasperated. "Stop saying Rick, Jasper!"

After a moment she stammers, "He was my best friend too. This has all been just... just unbearable. There's no right time, but I couldn't tell you at the funeral, and then you weren't going back, and we were settling back in together, struggling without him. But I always intended to tell you! I just, well I finally sucked it up today. Now you know."

"Marie." A plea. "You're telling me I've lost my two best friends at once."

"Oh Jasp. No! You'll never lose me. Never, never, never. I made a mistake. I'll work the rest of my life to unmake it! And Rick would have come around. You know it! Being a part of our family to the extent you wanted?? Fuck he was talking about himself! Working through the shock!"

Silence.

Mom, quietly, urgently, "Look, I want you to raise her as your own. I know it's a lot to ask! I know it's too much! But horrible as everything is, she's still a little piece of Rick for both of us to cherish. He'd want you to be her dad! And I want you to know, and still choose to do it! To be her Daddy!"

A pause, then almost inaudibly, "Her?"

Mom's urgency increases, "Yes! Jasper, another little girl! A little sister for Alice! Look, we should name her Susan, after your mother."

"Suzy." Jasper whispers.

"Yes, Suzy! And god forgive me for bribing you, but I want you to finish restoring that dumb old motorcycle Rick was working on. For Rick, and for our little Suzy."

Jasper, flatly, "My mother's name, and Rick's Indian Four, for fucking my best friend."

I feel Mom flinch. "Don't say it like that! You know it wasn't like that, and you can't think of Suzy that way! I, I loved Rick too, just like you did, but not in the same way that

I love you. Christ! Why isn't there a different word? I was confused! I made a mistake! Jasper, I'll never betray you again."

She sighs. "I know it's not a fair trade. I love you. I'm trying to make amends with everything I have."

"Jasper? Jasp?" plaintive. A pause. Resigned, she murmurs, "You'll have to decide how this plays out, from here."

A tense silence. Mom's heartbeat counts the time, steady, slowing, her quick shallow breaths beginning to deepen. It all seems to echo about me. We wait as one.

Finally he sighs too. "For Rick, and for Suzy. And you'll never leave. You love me."

I'm jostled lightly. I imagine Mom nodding intently, between tears and hope.

Quietly he mutters, "Goddamnit Marie."

I think he's going to say 'I love you too'. He wants to, I can feel it. Mom holds her breath briefly, then slowly blows it out.

The moment drags on.

The red glow dims, and the sensation of movement flows through me.

Distantly, I hear music. I imagine it's something magical, to escort me along, ferry me to the next stop on this strange journey. My curiosity burns as I strain to make it out. Slowly I recognize it's just Mom's favorite song. Played it all the time when I was a kid. Smiling, I remember her dancing all over the kitchen, belting out the lyrics, a glass of wine in hand. She'd grab me and we'd spin and spin, and just laugh, and laugh, and laugh.

There's the refrain, ah, I think it's called, "Old Orchard Beach". Whimsical, melancholy, jubilant, all rolled into a song. My mother, in verse.

Perfect. Thanks Mom. *The Wayward Bus* has come to bring me home, here at the end. Full circle.

And I'm ready to go. I love you.

The song fades. Content, I seem to float. Absently, I wonder if there'll be a light or something to head towards. I look around in anticipation, but of course I can't see anything. A giddy, light-heartedness envelopes me, and I try to suppress a giggle. It spills out in a heartly laugh as I shake my head and smile.

Thank you.

PART VI

Remember, remember, this is now, and now, and now.
Live it, feel it, cling to it.
I want to become acutely aware of all I've taken for granted.

The Unabridged Journals of Sylvia Plath, Sylvia Plath

1

I try to gasp. I can't! I am profoundly uncomfortable, and something is gagging me lightly. Suddenly air pours into my lungs, against my will! I try to gasp again, nothing! Noise all around, beeping. More forced air! I'm choking! I open my eyes. Too bright, blurry, I'm blind!

A male voice to my left, calm. "She's stacking breaths again. Looks like she's waking up. Does she need to be suctioned?"

Female, on the right. "Maybe. Press 100% for me? This is going to be uncomfortable my friend."

Suddenly I am choking on something, and worse, all the air is being sucked from my lungs. I gag violently.

Female again, "Cough, cough, cough, cough, cough. Good, good. Ok."

Male. "Didn't get much. Want me to call RT?"

"Nah, she looks feisty. I'll flip her to spontaneous, see how she does. If I have to put her back on a rate I'll have them come play with the settings."

The room is quiet for a second, then I take a deep breath! Another! Sweet Jesus.

Male. "Strong volumes. I like it. ICP still looks good. Be ready to put her down if it climbs though."

Annoyed, humoring, "Right. Of course. I'm good."

Sounding oblivious, his voice fades as he walks away, "Solid. Well let me know if you need anything. Oh, and ten's family made cookies, they're in the breakroom."

"Nice. Thanks." A quiet huff, then mumbling, "The ICP was back in range pretty quickly after suctioning Jeff. I've only been in neuro for ten years."

Footsteps in the room, water running for a moment. Suddenly a warm washcloth is wiping my eyelids. It is profoundly soothing in my miserable state. I let out a long sigh, and after a moment this pressure in my throat increases and stops me. A machine beeps nearby.

"You're ok. You're ok. Juuusstt getting some goop off your eyes. They were open a bit while you were sedated, so we've been gooping them up with ointment."

I blink and blink, and slowly the hospital room comes into focus. There's a tube down my throat, choking me a little but only if I move, and it's taped to my face which is somehow worse than the choking. There's a sharp pain in my forearm, my head aches, and I'm just generally uncomfortable, laying awkwardly on a bed, propped up on one side.

The woman is looking down at me. Mid-forties maybe, fit, narrow glasses across her pointed nose, prematurely greying hair pulled tightly into a no-nonsense bun. Kind eyes.

She smiles at me, making dimples pop up, "Hello there. You're in the ICU here in Missoula. You had a nasty fall, but you're doing much better now. This machine has been helping you breathe, but right now it's set for you to take your own breaths. It's simply providing enough pressure to mimic atmospheric pressure, so you're not breathing through a straw." Pointing to the tube in my throat.

I nod. I want to scratch my nose, but find my right arm is in a full cast, which is loosely tied to the bedframe, and my left wrist is tied to the other side. I try to move them both, Frankenstein-eske.

She frowns sympathetically, pats my hand, "That's standard. Every time someone wakes up they're confused and reach right for that tube to yank it out." She makes a clucking sound with her tongue, miming pulling a tube out of her mouth. "I would too! Can't have that though."

Taking my hand, "Can you squeeze my hand?" I squeeze. Leans across the bed and takes the fingers poking out of the cast. I squeeze as best I can. "Good, good." She goes down to the foot of the bed, grabs my feet. "Pull up against my hands. Ok. Push the gas. Excellent. Lift your head off the pillow? Nice!" I jazz hands in her general direction. She laughs.

The next few minutes include being poked and prodded a bit, the icy feel of her stethoscope, shining a light in my eyes, cleaning my teeth and the tube with mouthwash. I lay there, feeling helpless, distracted. A mental fog hangs about me, and I struggle to focus through the haze. How did I get here?

Coming back into my field of vision, she takes my hand again, pushing a few strands of hair out of my face with her other hand. "Your numbers are looking excellent. We might be able to pull that tube today. We'll see what the doc thinks shortly."

I hear her walk away, pause, walk back.

Looking down at me again she smiles broadly. "My name is Robin, I've been your nurse the last few days. It's so nice to finally meet you."

2

I drift in and out of sleep. People come and go. Machines beep. I lay there and ache.

Robin's cleaning my mouth again. "Rounds will be by in a few minutes, try to wake up and listen." She turns to throw something away. "I know you're uncomfortable, but can I do anything?"

I gesture at the tube in my throat as best I can with my hands tied. She smiles and shakes her head. I shrug.

Pulling the sheet under my hips, she faces me more towards the door, and I shift around in the bed a little. She fixes my pillow, points to her ear, and hustles out.

A few minutes later there's a group of people standing in and around the double door, some in slacks but most in scrubs. A tall, fifty something man with bushy eyebrows overhanging his thick glasses, wearing a narrow tie in addition to slacks, appears to be running the show. He stands at a computer attached to a small table with wheels at the bottom, like a mobile podium. An attractive, bright eyed girl wearing a lab coat stands at his side, and they are engrossed in the content on the screen. Everyone else is watching them, waiting.

The man looks up at the group, "I'm going to have Jennifer run rounds for this patient today, and feel free to grill her a little. Got to give residents a win sometimes! That Ok Robin?" He has a slight English lilt. Robin crinkles her eyes lightly, nods.

Shuffling some papers in her hands, the girl in the lab coat smiles at the group, "This is Jane Doe, estimated,"

The man holds up a hand, interrupts, "Where's Social Work?" A pause. "No Social Work today?" Looking around at the people in the group, a few shaking their heads. With a small sigh he turns to my nurse. "Robin, any progress on her identity?"

Robin shakes her head, "Last I heard police had checked all the nearby trailheads, no abandoned cars, and no one has been reported missing. It's presumed she ran quite a distance, probably lives up there somewhere. They're willing to start canvasing the homes within a reasonable radius, but we're holding off in hopes of just asking her soon."

The man looks in at me, and I raise my eyebrows. "Ok, yeah I think we'll resolve that mystery today." He turns back to his resident.

She looks a little flustered, but smiles again, "Estimated twenty to twenty-five years old, maybe older given her fitness, found down times unknown number of days after a fall in a remote area. Per EMS, she must have tumbled forty or fifty feet down a steep grade, then free fallen about thirty into a rocky ravine. Pretty beat up, but most significantly she sustained a TBI[1] and a clean, closed fracture of the right ulna and radius."

---

[1] Part VI, Chapter 2a 'A Brief, Unofficial Index of Medical Jargon' is available if desired

Pausing she looks up. Nobody says anything and the man cocks his head at her. She continues, "Right wrist involvement as well. EMS started two Liters of NS bilaterally before moving her, due to the risk of rhabdo and compartment syndrome, but given the lengthy extraction her QRS had widened significantly and heart rate dropped into the twenties by time they got her to the copter. Intubated during take-off, with one round of pulseless VTach times 128 seconds in route, ROSC achieved by shock times two, EPI times one, with high quality CPR."

She looks around again, takes a deep breath, "In flight the ER doc radioed orders for Insulin and D50, switching fluids to BiCarb, for presumed hyperkalemia, but on arrival K was still 7.6 with minimal urine production. Nephro initiated CRRT for persistent hyperkalemia with EKG changes, but discontinued it after only six hours as both stabilized and urine output increased dramatically. It is believed kidney involvement was secondary to profound dehydration rather than the onset of rhabdo, and CK levels have been high but trending down."

She side-eyes Robin, who subtly taps the side of her head. The resident clears her throat and dives back in, "During this time neuro was consulted given the gash on the back of her head. They placed an EVD and ICP was found to be elevated. Per recommendation she's been heavily sedated and hyperventilated due to the ICP, but my understanding is it's been consistently within normal limits since placement of the drain, and the plan was to wake her this morning."

Robin chimes in. "Chip titrated her fentanyl down through the night, and he turned it off around 0500. I had the propofol off by 0730. Waking up, she had a lot of trouble with the ventilator, stacking breaths, trying to force her own rate, depth, fighting it, but she's been cruising on spontaneous. She's pretty awake and alert in there, follows commands, moves all extremities well, appears to understand what's going on."

Everybody turns and looks at me. I feel pretty exposed in my little hospital gown, but I jazz hands anyway, garnering quite a chuckle from the group.

The man comes in and takes my hand, "Give me a good squeeze."

I squeeze as hard as I can and he smiles. Laughing, he turns to the group, "Ouch! Yeah, I think we can just yank everything out of her this morning. Jennifer? Invasive lines?"

The girl comes over to the bed as well, "Right. Tubed with OG, EVD, Foley, Trialysis Catheter, Central Line, A-Line."

Robin pipes up from behind her, "No Central Line. She never needed pressors, plus we've got the pigtail on the Trialysis."

The man turns to the girl, "Any significant events you might have forgotten?"

She stares blankly, and someone I can't see coughs, "O.R."

She smiles, "Right, Neuro gave the go ahead to ortho yesterday, and she went to the O.R. for a reduction and internal fixation of her right arm and wrist. Got some nice hardware in there now."

He returns her smile, nods, looks around at the group. "Great job everybody. This is going to be a real win." Turning to me he pats my arm, "Any longer out there..." Shakes his head, "It was dicey when you got here, but you've been in great hands since! I'm Dr. Alford, the ICU doctor managing your care. You're doing great."

He looks back up at the group. "Questions?"

Robin steps over, "We're still giving her 150 an hour of D10. Want to D/c it?"

He scratches his chin, "No edema? Lungs still sound ok? Lots of urine? Stable glucose?" Robin nods repeatedly. "I'm fine with that, but it can't hurt to leave it going, given her CK levels. Ask nephro when they come by."

Someone else standing with one of those computer carts pipes up, "We're still hitting her with Zosyn prophylactically. Never any signs of infection."

Dr. Alford points at him, "Right. D/c it."

He looks around. No one else says anything. He directs his attention to the machine next to my bed, gestures at the girl.

She studies the screen for a moment, then says, "Great volumes, rate, minute ventilation, effort. No brainer."

Smiling down at me, he pats my arm again, "We're going to take that tube out of your throat shortly. I'm just going to give you a little more time to process all the sedatives you've been getting."

Turning back to the group, "Extubation after we finish rounds. Robin, get neuro to pull that EVD ASAP, she doesn't need it. Once that's out pull the foley. Trialysis and A-Line too."

He claps his hands. "Man that's a fast recovery! Someone get a PSA going about making all our patients runners!"

A few scattered chuckles as everyone files out of the room. Robin smiles at me on her way out.

Fleetingly, I wonder if anyone paused my Garmin, saving the run.

2a

A Brief, Unofficial Index of Medical Jargon

A-Line: Arterial Line, a small tube inserted into a peripheral artery, commonly in the wrist, to measure blood pressure continuously in real time.

BiCarb: Sodium BiCarbonate, a standard IV fluid, generally used to treat a pH imbalance (acidosis, specifically). Acidosis can be caused by high potassium.

Bilaterally: Both sides of the body.

Central Line: A large multiport IV used to administer caustic medications or high-volume IV fluids.

CK levels: Creatine Kinase levels, an enzyme found in muscle tissue that circulates in the blood stream after muscle breakdown, serving as a measure for the risk of rhabdomyolysis.

Clean, closed fracture: The bone broke cleanly, rather than shattering into little pieces, and the bone did not protrude through the skin.

Compartment Syndrome: High pressure in a limited area of the body, generally resulting from injury, a lack of movement, or both, restricting blood flow to the area and causing tissue death. Can cause or enhance Rhabdomyolysis. When the pressure is released, the massive influx of dead cellular waste into the blood stream can overwhelm the body and rapidly be fatal.

CPR: Cardiopulmonary Resuscitation, manually pressing the chest in an attempt to force the heart to compress and distribute blood to the body.

CRRT: Continuous Renal Replacement Therapy, a machine used in ICU to replace the function of kidneys, namely cleaning metabolic waste from the bloodstream, removing excess fluid, balancing electrolytes (including potassium) and balancing pH (body acidity or alkalinity).

D10: A standard IV fluid containing a small amount of dextrose (sugar).

D50: A medication with a high concentration of dextrose (sugar), often used to increase blood sugar rapidly, but also used in conjunction with Insulin to temporarily force excess potassium out of the blood stream.

Edema: Fluid collection in bodily tissues, often causing swelling in extremities such as legs, feet and hands.

Effort: A calculation on a ventilator, indicating how hard the patient is working to achieve adequate breathing.

EKG: Electrocardiogram, a tracing of the electrical activity within the heart, utilized to evaluate the effectiveness and nature of individual heartbeats. Sometimes called ECG.

EMS: Emergency Medical Services

EPI: Epinephrine, a drug used to stimulate the heart when it is not beating effectively.

EVD: Extra-ventricular Drain, a tube placed into the ventricles of the brain, a fluid filled space, to drain excess fluid after a head injury, inhibiting brain swelling from causing further damage due to the limited space within the skull, as there is no room to swell.

Extubation: Removing an endotracheal tube, and thereby freeing the patient from a ventilator.

Fentanyl: A powerful opioid medication, for comfort and pain control during sedation.

Foley: Foley Catheter, a tube inserted through the urethra to the bladder to drain urine into a collection bag.

Hyperkalemia: High potassium, potentially causing heart dysrhythmias and increasingly fatal at higher levels.

ICP: Intracranial Pressure, the pressure inside the skull, measured by an EVD, which causes brain damage or death as it increases.

Insulin: A medication given to reduce blood sugar, but also used in conjunction with D50 to temporarily force excess potassium out of the blood stream.

Intubated: Endotracheal intubation, placing a tube in the throat in order to deliver oxygen directly to the lungs.

K: The chemical symbol for Potassium. Potassium regulates heart rhythm and is fatal when too high (or too low).

Minute Ventilation: The total volume of air a patient moves in one minute, a measure of breathing effectiveness on a ventilator.

Nephro: Nephrologist, a kidney specialist.

Neuro: Neurologist, a brain specialist.

NS: Normal Saline, a standard IV fluid.

OG: Orogastric tube, a tube inserted into the mouth of an intubated patient leading to the stomach, temporarily utilized for oral medication administration, tube feedings, or gastric decompression (draining the stomach contents).

Ortho: Orthopedics, a bone specialist.

Pigtail: See *Trialysis Catheter*.

'Press 100%': A button on a ventilator that temporarily delivers 100% oxygen (room air is only 21%), to provide extra oxygen to a patient if needed, often used in conjunction with suctioning.

Pressors: A class of caustic IV medications utilized to constrict vessels and increase blood pressure.

Prophylactically: Preventatively.

Propofol: A sedating medication, utilized to keep an intubated patient unconscious and comfortable while on a ventilator.

QRS: The QRS complex is a component of the electrical activity of each heartbeat, which can be dangerous or fatal as it widens.

Reduction and Internal Fixation: Reduction is placing the bones together in the correct alignment, and fixation is securing them together with rods, plates, and screws. Fixation can be internal, usually permanent, or in more severe cases external to the body, which are later removed after sufficient healing.

Rhabdo: Rhabdomyolysis, a potentially fatal condition caused by muscle breakdown occurring faster than the body can process the resulting cellular waste, causing severe kidney damage. Extreme exercise, dehydration, and denying muscles oxygen by not moving and/or releasing pressure, or some combination of all three, are usual causes of Rhabdo.

ROSC: Return of Spontaneous Circulation, when the heart begins beating appropriately again, effectively distributing blood to the body.

Rounds: An interdisciplinary team of healthcare workers gathering to discuss each patient, at minimum including the attending physician, patient's nurse, respiratory therapist, and pharmacist. Numerous other disciplines join as appropriate/available, such as social worker, dietitian, discharge planner, medical residents, physician assistants, charge nurse, nursing students, nurse manager. Specialty physicians such as neurology (brain), nephrology (kidney), orthopedics (bone), etc. generally round on patients solo on their own schedule.

RT: Respiratory therapist, who manages ventilator settings in conjunction with the physician in an ICU setting, as well as lungs, breathing, and respiratory medications throughout the hospital.

Spontaneous: A setting on a ventilator where a patient is doing all their own breathing, and only receiving minimal support from the ventilator.

Stacking Breaths: A patient trying to force their own breaths over the breaths provided by the ventilator, resulting in getting both in succession and out of rhythm, creating discomfort and hyperventilation. Commonly occurs when a patient is not tolerating the ventilator and needs different settings or increased sedation.

Suctioning: A tiny tube located inside an endotracheal tube that can extend to the base of the lungs, utilized to suction secretions directly out of the lungs. Ventilated patients cannot cough up their natural secretions effectively, and often have excess secretions depending on their reason for needing mechanical ventilation.

TBI: Traumatic Brain Injury. Generally assumed with any significant head injury.

Trialysis Catheter: A large multiport catheter similar to an IV, inserted into a large vein to access the bloodstream for renal replacement therapy. Also has an extra port, commonly called a pigtail, that is smaller and can be used for caustic IV medications.

Tubed: See *Intubated*.

Ulna and Radius: The two bones in the forearm.

VTach: Ventricular Tachycardia, a fast-paced cardiac dysrhythmia that is ineffective in distributing blood and therefore fatal.

Zosyn: A broad spectrum antibiotic, often utilized when an infection is presumed but the causative bacteria, and therefore antibiotic effectiveness, is unknown.

3

The next few days passed in a blur. They moved me to a regular hospital room, keeping me to watch for concussion symptoms and monitor my labs.

I signed a paper that lets me go outside for half an hour at a time, a policy nicotine forced upon the hospital, as apparently too many smokers leave against doctor's orders when prohibited from indulging their habit. Thanks to them I am generally a free-range patient. I've never felt so weak as I did that first day, and I spend most of my time walking the halls and heading outside when they let me.

As soon as they took that damn tube out of my throat I told them about Samson, the poor kitty probably starving at home, and a nurse actually agreed to check on him after their shift! He had drunk most of the toilet water, but otherwise seemed fine. The nurse lives out near my place, has been dropping in on him daily, and even gathered a few items for me from the house.

My memory of the day I fell is hazy at best, and nothing beyond getting ready for the run, but I was in the ICU for three days before they woke me, and after charging my Garmin I discovered it automatically saved the run when the battery died. It recorded twelve miles, and it's dated five days before I was found!

Everyone was shocked to hear it was so long, and the general consensus is my runner's cardiac endurance played a role in my survival. It's weird to wonder whether I just lay there helpless, or if I valiantly struggled to climb out of the ravine, but my memory's blank, more than a week of my life, gone!

I asked Dr. Alford about it. He told me the concussion could have kept me unconscious for a while, allowing severe dehydration to make me too hypotensive for any real conscious awareness, especially given the long run beforehand. But then he spread his hands and said it's normal to have memory impairment around any traumatic event, especially involving the brain, and shrugged.

I was about to accept it as a complete mystery, but he continued to think out loud while looking over my chart, mumbling that I probably would have developed more advanced rhabdo if I hadn't moved at all for so many days. On his way out he winked, pointing out that five days unconscious in the mountains is an awfully long time to avoid animal interest, so I was surely fighting them off left and right.

That was enough to tip the scales for me, and I've decided I spent the time waving a log around with my good arm, a pack of wolves biting at my heels! Absolutely everyone keeps saying I'm lucky to be alive though. That I know.

I called mom, and had to argue at length to keep her from flying out here immediately. Finally I agreed to come visit when they release me, and she's all aflutter setting me up with physical therapy for my wrist there in Asheville. In truth, I can't wait to head back east.

Waking up in the ICU is a sobering experience, and I'm left with the impression my life has been off track for some time now.

I didn't tell mom, but I'm not certain I even want to come back to Montana. It's beautiful out here, and I love my little home. I mean, the view brings me so much peace every morning, and it's simply a wonderful place to write, but it's just not enough. Something is missing! Maybe my next book will allow me to keep it as a vacation home, my tiny retreat in the mountains, and I could come out to write for a month from time to time. I hang on to this idea. It's soothing.

Most importantly, ever since I came to I've been thinking about my two best friends from childhood, Rachel and Ethan. And I mean, constantly! They've never been far from my mind, but I suppose having a near death experience puts things into a new light. Every time I wonder what they look like today, or how they're doing, or if they think of me, I have this surge of emotion! My god I just want to hug them both!

Oy, I asked mom to get their numbers, she's still friends with their parents, and I am terrified! I've thought about calling them so many times over the years, and for the first time I'm actually going to do it. It feels so good to finally be taking this step! I betrayed them both, and I don't know what I'm going to say, but 'Hello' seems like a good start.

4

A knock on the door interrupts my reverie.

"Sure, come on in." checking that my hospital gown is covering me.

A girl walks in, about my age, dressed in a tan uniform, thick curly hair up in a short pony tail. She looks a bit uncomfortable, standing awkwardly, taking in the room slowly before staring at me a moment.

She starts to extend her hand to shake, but stops, uncertain, "Uh. Hello, I'm Lauren. I work for the Forest Service. I found you in the ravine."

I smile and offer my hand. We shake, "Hi Lauren, I'm Susan. Thank you for saving my life." It feels formal and weird.

She blushes, looks at my feet a second. "I, uh, I threw up on you. I'm sorry."

This breaks the ice, and I burst out laughing. She chuckles quietly with me. Smiling, I tell her, "Well I'll let it slide, what with the life-saving and all."

Still chuckling lightly, she points at the guest chair in my room, "Do you mind if I sit for a minute? My boyfriend insisted I come see you. Not that I didn't want to see you! Uh, I wasn't sure it'd be appropriate is all. But it was just a bit traumatizing I guess, and he said you're doing so well, and would be interested to meet me. He's a kidney nurse, he set up your CRRT machine when you got here."

I do know her boyfriend, "Right, he's the one checking on Samson." I don't know why she didn't mention him that way.

She smiles broadly, "That's him! He says Samson is a really sweet kitty. Actually I was going to ask if you minded, if I could go see him too. We don't have a cat."

Ah, I suppose she didn't want it to sound like she had a cat related agenda. I almost laugh as I realize that, it's simply too cute, endearing. I like her immediately.

"Certainly, he'd love that. I'd love that!"

She eases back into the chair, eyes wandering the room again, scratches her neck idly. "I was down in the ravine doing a survey, looking for insect damage to the trees." Looks up at me, eyes wide, "I thought you were dead! You were so pale, leaves strewn across your body."

Shuddering a little, she continues, "I ran up to you and the second I saw your arm, bent right in the middle at this crazy angle!" She holds her arms out as if pushing me away and makes a face. "Well, I couldn't decide if I was going to puke or pass out, so I did both!"

She laughs hard now, and it's my turn to chuckle quietly with her.

Leaning towards me she turns the right side of her forehead my direction, and I see a handful of stiches near her hairline.

"I was in the ER about to get stitched up when Leif had to leave. He got called right then to set up your CRRT!"

I smile at the timing, "Wow, sorry about that!"

Laughing, she waves this off, "No, of course that was fine! Actually I was glad he got to go be part of your care. I was so worried about you, it made me feel better, as if by braving the stiches alone I was helping you too."

I nod appreciatively, not certain how to respond.

She leans back in the chair again. "Anyway, I came to, lying across your belly, my head on a rock, my puke on your shirt, and that's when I realized you were actually breathing! It was subtle, but I could feel the slight rise beneath me! Immediately fumbled for my radio and pressed the emergency button. Never had to do that before."

She grabs a walkie-talkie looking handheld off her belt, and shows me a red button under a little cover.

"There wasn't much for me to do after that. They got an ER doctor on the radio who had me check your pulse and count your breaths, try to gently wake you, but they didn't want me to move you or anything. Plus I was bleeding quite a bit myself." Gesturing broadly to the right side of her face and shirt, "I could have been an extra in a horror movie!"

Shaking her head, bemused. "Took almost two hours for the EMS people to get down there to us. Longest two hours of my life."

We sit in silence for a moment, Lauren staring out the window, me imagining the whole scene, both lost in it.

She stands to go, and I stand too, suddenly pulling her into a big hug! It's awkward at first, but you can't go through something like that together and still be strangers. I feel a real spark of human connection as we relax into the hug together. Lauren's rubbing my back and sniffling a little, which makes me tear up too. We hold each other for a few minutes.

Finally she breaks the hug, holding me gently at arm's length. Locking eyes with me she nods, "I'm so happy you're ok Susan."

Smiling broadly, "Me too. Thank you Lauren."

She walks out, and after a second I pop out into the hallway too, "Lauren?"

She turns, eyebrows up.

"I'd like to keep in touch. You know, Christmas cards or something at least! Can I have your address?"

I've caught her off guard, and she hesitates, probably trying to decide if it's proper.

Before she can respond I put my hands up, "Wait, I've put you on the spot. Let me give you my number, then you can text me your address later if you want. No pressure!"

She smiles, processes for a moment, says, "I'd like that." and hands me her phone to type it in.

She watches me do it, and as I'm handing back the phone she smiles again, looking a little shy. "Actually Leif and I are both runners too..." She trails off, shrugs, lets the implication hang.

I haven't made many friends since I moved to Montana, so naturally right when I'm thinking about leaving! Course I don't recommend meeting people this way. I nod and smile, making a little 'call me' gesture with my hand next to my ear.

She laughs and waves goodbye.

⊰ও ৯⊱

I'm lying there imagining what it must have been like to find me in the ravine like that, when another knock startles me. You really don't get any peace in a hospital! Sighing, I try to sound chipper, "Come on in!"

Another uniform, this one blue, tries to contain a woman with a buzz cut, who strides in like she owns the room. The short sleeves are rolled slightly, like we're in the fifties, and she has bigger biceps than most men I know. Definitely ex-military. She stares at me.

After a moment she breaks into a boisterous laugh and slaps the plastic footboard of my bed, "You look amazing!"

I'm a little intimidated, but that doesn't seem to be her intention, so I smile up at her, offering an, "Uh, thanks!"

She grabs the plastic guest chair and flips it around, straddling it with her arms resting on the back. "I'm Roxanne, but you can call me Roxy. I'm the flight nurse who brought you here in the chopper!"

Oh. Well this seems an appropriate visit after Lauren's. Polar opposites though. Increasingly I get the impression I'm a small celebrity with the way I've recovered. Basically the entire ICU came to see me before they moved me to this room.

Trying to match her enthusiasm, I manage a, "Well hey Roxy! Thanks for keeping me alive!"

She looks serious for a second, "You're not kidding. You were a scary one! I hate doing CPR on the chopper." Then she smiles again. "Look, I've got a question."

I raise my eyebrows, having no idea where this is going.

She points at me, almost aggressively, "Are you a writer?"

I try to hide my shock. Did this Amazon really read my book and actually recognize me from the book jacket or something? She's a far cry from the audience I pictured, but I'm excited to meet my first fan! "I am! Did you read my book?"

Frowning, she furrows her prominent brow, "No."

I mirror her expression. Dumb question I guess. I wait silently.

After a moment she dismisses the question and smiles, "Well I'm trying to be a writer, action, high drama!" She makes a little machine gun noise and mimes spraying the room with gunfire. "And I'm taking a class at the U. It's boring, but I figure I need to do the legwork, just like nursing school. Anyway, right as we took off, your heart rate in the twenties, I'm getting ready to intubate you and you're busy getting ready to code on me! The take-off was rough, kind of at an angle, and your head lolled to the side a little in the neck brace." She puts her hands around her neck, like the brace I suppose, and lolls her head to the side, one eye half open, fluttering, tongue hanging out. It's quite the visual.

"I swear take-off jostled you awake, I watched your heart rate pop up slightly, a lively thirty-five! You mumbled something, staring out the window, but no one believes me, given your condition and the sound of the rotors! You being a writer proves it!" She jumps up and flexes, laughing.

I can't help but laugh with her. She is one enthusiastic adrenaline junkie, and I am suddenly immensely grateful people like her exist, flying around in helicopters, saving people's lives. "What did I say?"

She looks down at me, "We talked about it in class that same week, and given the chopper and everything, it was perfect!"

I raise my eyebrows as high as I can, "Roxy? What was it?"

She laughs again, then shakes her head. "Deus Ex Machina."

5

They plan to discharge me tomorrow morning, as long as my AM labs come back as expected, and I've already bought a one-way ticket to Asheville for next week.

Trying to make the most of my last night at the hospital, not to mention the thirty minutes I'm permitted to be outside, me and my cafeteria pizza are taking in the sunset from a bench in a little garden area. I will most definitely miss these western sunsets, painting the mountains in oranges, pinks and reds, tonight sporting an epic, multilayered cloud cover too. I sigh. Big sky indeed.

A little old lady is heading my way, using a cane but still looking pretty spry. I try not to make eye contact, hoping to enjoy some peace and quiet away from the hospital, but she stops right next to me anyway.

Tapping her cane on the bench, "Mind if I join you dear?"

Suppressing a different sort of sigh, I decide it's fine, she seems sweet. I smile at her, "Certainly. Take a look at this sunset!"

She sits quietly, her hands resting on the cane cradled between her legs, staring at the colors while I munch my pizza. It's a companionable silence. I chastise myself for wishing she would leave me alone. Sometimes people just need a little company at a hospital.

After a few minutes, without looking away from the sunset, she says simply, "You're Jane Doe."

I pause mid-bite, surprised, as I had imagined she was someone's family member. Around the too large bite I mumble, "I am, or was. I'm Susan."

She looks at my hands, notes the grease, and pats me on the leg instead of shaking, "Nice to meet you Susan, I'm June."

She's quiet again, long enough for me to wonder if she'll elaborate on her role in ICU. I elect not to ask and go back to enjoying my pizza sunset.

Once I've finished eating she looks at me again, taking me in as I wipe my hands on the hospital scrubs my nurse gave me. "We had a moment in ICU, you and I. I wasn't certain you'd want to know the gory details, but I saw you sitting here and Bernie forced me to come over."

She looks back out at the sunset, wearing a half smile which immediately makes me think of Rachel. I have that little surge of emotion in my stomach again! I lean back, both nervous and happy with the idea that I'll be calling her soon.

June taps her cane on the ground a few times, "Bernie is my late husband you see, his ghost is always nudging me around."

I'm not certain if she's kidding or crazy, and I offer a non-committal, "Hm."

She laughs, poking my foot with her cane, "It's very convenient. All the time I'm just, 'Bernie, why'd you make me buy this candy bar?' or 'Bernie, why'd you make me watch TV all day?'" She side-eyes me, "Or 'Bernie, why'd you make me bother this nice girl who just wanted to enjoy a sunset in peace?'"

Relieved, I laugh. "He does sound like a bit of a pest!"

She smiles at me, "You're telling me. Always was. Some things never change."

She's quiet a moment, and I can tell she's pondering what she wants to say. It's getting chilly with dusk, and I pull my puffy jacket a little tighter around the scrubs, grateful Leif brought it from my house.

Sitting up a little straighter, tapping her cane once, "I'm a volunteer. I spend most of my time talking to lonely people my age in their rooms, trying to provide a little much needed companionship while they're here."

She looks at me, "I like spending time in the ICU though, with the unconscious or sedated patients. Most of the staff talk over them or around them, throwing medical jargon all over the place, or even just gossiping about their day. Makes the patient into a thing instead of a person. They're just doing a job, might as well be repairing a car."

I could see that. I don't remember being treated like a thing, but I guess I was sedated.

Frowning, she continues, "I try to combat that. I like to sit in the room and talk to them. Tell then what's going on, in my layman terms, or simply ask them how they're doing as if they can respond. I think they can hear. Sometimes I just sit and hold their hand."

She pats me on the leg again, "You may not know it, but you had two tubes in your throat, the one for breathing and another going into your stomach, for medications and that yellow goop they were feeding you. It's like Ensure I guess, but your stomach didn't like it! I expect mine wouldn't either."

Grimacing, tapping her cane again, a nervous habit. "Well I'm in there talking to you, and Robin decides to suction your lungs out, making you gag! That was the tipping point for your poor stomach, and abruptly all that yellow goop came pouring out of your mouth! Caused a hub-bub, more nurses running in, turning you on your side, flipping on that bright overhead light, someone yelling about the tube coming from the back of your head, a big mess! But I was holding your hand, which they had to untie to turn you, and you hung on to me for dear life." She looks down at her hand, turning it over, "I had bruises on the back after. Looks a little better now."

Reaching over she takes my hand, paper thin skin, reminding me of my grandmother. Her hand still looks pretty bruised to me. I give her a squeeze, "I'm sorry."

She looks at me, mouth slightly agape, "You're missing the point dear! I'm trying to thank you. My time in the ICU is a thankless job, and with you I felt like I really helped!" She blinks once, "So thank you."

Right. I smile, "No, thank *you*. You did help."

She shrugs, letting go of my hand, turns back to the now dusky sky. "Brace yourself. I did come over here with an agenda."

I'm amused. She is like Gram. "Oh?"

Smacks my leg with her cane. A little harder than she intended I think, and I try not to flinch. "Robin told me you cried a lot, unusual under all that sedation. Chip kept turning your Fentanyl up, thinking you were in pain, but she and I thought different." She nods once, decisively, "It was emotional distress."

I frown lightly, embarrassed, but immediately think of Rachel and Ethan, again accompanied by that little surge of emotion. "You might be right. I've done nothing but think of my two best friends from childhood since I woke up. We had a falling out."

She makes a little fist pump, a bit incongruous against her calm, elderly demeanor. "I knew it." Pauses a beat, then locks eyes with me. "Waking up in ICU is a new lease on life, and a great excuse to sever ties with the old you, turn over a new leaf. You're going to call them." A statement, not a question.

Deciding not to be offended by the command, I nod. "I'm scared, but I'm doing it. Actually flying home next week, planning to stay for a while, hoping to see them."

I hold up a hand, fingers crossed.

She pats me on the knee one more time, stands up, agenda accomplished. "I'm sure you will dear."

She's already walking away and I wave at her back, "It was nice to meet you June. Thanks again!"

She holds up a hand over her shoulder, but then stops, turning back towards me, "What are you going to do with Samson?"

I laugh, suddenly realizing this little old lady must be an excellent source for hospital gossip. I spread my hands, "Haven't figured that one out yet, kitty carrier I guess."

Poking her cane at me, "On a cross country flight? No. Ask Leif. He's a sweet boy. We used to be neighbors, and he got me this job after Bernie died. He and Lauren will take care of Samson as long as you need."

She smiles to herself, and I can see the gears of a busybody turning, "Actually, they're living in a Yurt up there while building their dream home, but it's taking too long and the Yurt will be too cold for Lauren soon. I bet they'd rent your place, if you wanted."

I smile and nod. There's no way I'd impose on them like that. I watch her walk off, and wonder if she even needs the cane, or just uses it to tap and poke people, a prop to make points.

It's dark now, clearly breaking the thirty-minute rule, but I take one more long moment to revel in the impression I've just enjoyed a sunset with my grandmother. My limited memory of Gram is much the same, a busybody in the sweetest way possible. Feeling content, I laugh. I haven't thought of her in years! Heading in, I wonder if I can find a peppermint somewhere in the hospital.

6

Sure enough, I'm at home packing the next afternoon when I get a text from Lauren, checking on me, but mainly asking if I'd like them to take care of Samson while I'm gone. June meddles quickly! We went back and forth, 'I can't impose!' 'We love Samson!' 'It's too much to ask!' 'We insist!' etc. and finally we made arrangements for me to bring him to their Yurt tomorrow.

It's quite close actually, and I wonder if renting my place will come up too. I'm planning to offer it free if so, as long as it's month to month. I can survive my childhood home all the way through winter, and then they can go back to their Yurt, or their new dream home if it's finished. Six or seven months back in good ol' Asheville sounds like plenty of time to figure out my next steps.

Plus, while I hate the idea of selling, I know my place would fetch a better price in the Spring. I'll bring Rachel and Ethan out here first of course, their girlfriends too if they have them. I smile, my little home suddenly feeling full of life for the first time. It's a good plan.

Mom called. Physical therapy for my wrist is arranged, the same person she went to after dislocating her knee, and he's 'simply fabulous.' I have an orthopedic appointment here tomorrow, follow-up with the surgeon who repaired my forearm, but then I'm free to go.

After this whole ordeal, it feels a bit unreal. A little PT, regrow some hair where they stitched up my head, well, my accident will be ancient history. My hair is probably too thick for the twelve stitches to leave a visible scar, which is almost disappointing. I'd wear it with pride, a reminder of my wake-up call! All told, I am eternally grateful to be coming out the other side unscathed, and ready to make some life changes.

Speaking of life changes, mom also arranged a 'Welcome Home, Congratulations on Not Dying' party, and already invited Ethan's mom and Rachel's parents, a not so subtle message I'm to invite them as well. I know she envisions a future of gatherings like this one, backyard barbeques with all of us and our families, she the matriarch, sitting with her friends of twenty plus years, surrounded by children and grandchildren. A scene she first dreamed up when the three of us became inseparable. I'm glad there aren't any grandchildren yet, but I share her excitement and my heart aches to believe in it!

⤙⤚

Wrapped in a blanket, rocking gently on my porch swing, I try to absorb the view into every part of my body, the emotion of leaving this place threatening to drown me. I sigh. No, that's an excuse. I am sad about Montana, but that's not why I'm drowning.

I roll my neck around, count ten slow, deep breaths, and finally acknowledge my phone, sitting there in my slightly shaking hand, Rachel's name pulled up in the contacts.

Closing my eyes, I think of doing some silly dance, spinning, Ethan's goofy smile, taking up his entire face, Rachel bursting into infections laughter that spreads between us like wildfire, and I try to imagine what they look like now, try to picture the same scene as adults.

Looking down at Rachel's name again, I imagine hugging them next week, and the idea fills me with happiness. I hold the phone to my chest as a few tears escape down my cheeks.

I press the call button.

It rings.

Rings.

"Suzy?"

Her voice! Unmistakable, quiet, hopeful. Time collapses as I catch my breath! A wave of emotion swells, a firework blossoming from my chest outward, making my fingers and toes tingle.

Suddenly I realize I'm no longer nervous, and I straighten up. I know how she felt all those years ago. I know how she feels now. I know.

Connected, loved, loving.

I close my eyes, roll it all into a neat little package as I breathe her name.

"Rachel."

EPILOGUE

We are the music makers,
And we are the dreamers of dreams,
Wandering by lone sea-breakers,
And sitting by desolate streams; —
World-losers and world-forsakers,
On whom the pale moon gleams

"Ode", Arthur O'Shaughnessy

Cradling three beers awkwardly with my cast against my chest, I stop for a double take in front of the fireplace.

You Are Here
All Who Seek
All Who Wander
-- And Wonder --
You Are Welcome

With my other hand I grab the bag of chips clutched between my teeth, "Mom? Where did you get this sign?"

She pops her head in from the kitchen, smiling wide. "I made it. It's for you sweetie! I'm so glad you noticed it today of all days! It was my little project, nursing the hope that my wanderer would come home. And here you are!"

Frowning a moment, she studies the sign. "Actually, I wouldn't have if I'd known how it was going to happen." Shrugs, smiles again.

Looking from her to the sign, I have a massive rush of déjà vu. "You made this? It's incredible! I love the quote!"

She blushes a little, "Well I *designed* it. Jasper carved it and stained it and all." Seeing my grimace, she continues, "He knew it was about you honey."

Whatever. "Did you write the quote too? I'm certain I recognize it."

Mom actually jazz hands at me, all too familiar. "Yours truly!" Then raising an eyebrow my way, "It was in Jasper's workshop the last time you were here, partly done. Maybe you spotted it there?"

I nod, the feeling of déjà vu dissipating. I generally avoid the workshop, but did go in there last summer in search of batteries for my headlamp.

Facing the blank TV to squint at my faint reflection, I put the chips back between my teeth to free a hand and adjust my hair buff, make sure the bald spot with my stiches is covered. I feel a little like the ghost I see silhouetted in the black screen. Back from the dead, heading into a new world, or maybe into the past. Both.

I stop again at the glass door, arrested by the overwhelming emotions hanging all about. Everything is surreal. There they are. Rachel and Ethan sitting in a couple of lawn chairs out by Mom's maple tree, laughing.

It seems incongruous seeing them there in my childhood backyard again. Their interaction, mannerisms, body language, so familiar, comforting, safe, I could describe the scene with my eyes closed! But it strongly feels they should be children. Like I was staring into my past, blinked and somehow skipped twenty years! Everything has changed, yet somehow remained the same. And it needs to be the same. I need it! For a moment opening the door is truly terrifying.

Confident they can't see me, I watch for a minute, soaking it in. I catch my breath, marveling at the past week.

❧

Rachel convinced Mom to let her surprise me at the airport. Dropping my bag, I burst out crying the moment I saw her! We just held each other sobbing like idiots until some parking attendant insisted she move the car. I will never understand why I thought it would be so difficult to reconnect.

Ethan was harder. I was so much worse to him, but mainly it was his blunt honesty, and I am truly grateful for it.

We met at our favorite coffee shop, graduating from the hot chocolates we ordered as teenagers to actual coffee. It was awkward at first, but suddenly he poked me on the nose, offering my own 'suck it up, buttercup', and gently placing a peppermint next to my cup.

I am in awe of the man he has become, and the gentle insight now complimenting his giant smile, as though his head caught up with his heart. He doesn't hold it against me. I messed up his relationships for years, but he forgave me in college, evidently after gaining an appreciation for my fear of vulnerability, and how sex overwhelmed and blinded me. He actually thanked me for driving him to study psychology, for helping him find his purpose! I told him he was just making excuses on my behalf.

He shook his head, shrugging, and said 'We can't change what happens to us, but we can do our best to choose how we react. I reacted by learning about it, and forgiving my best friend.'

Then he smiled broadly, telling me it was crucial I came around to forgiving myself on my own, and he was so relieved, so happy, to see I was finally ready to. At this he suddenly grabbed my hand, eyes wet but aglow, and said I had his permission to do so, but didn't need it, I held the key.

This was too much too fast, turning me into an embarrassing blubbering mess right then and there in my chair. But it felt good. It feels good. Cathartic.

✦✦

Staring though the glass door at my two oldest friends, I'm lost, unable to believe this reality. I'd pinch myself if it wasn't so awkward with the cast, beers, and chips. It's too important! Shifting my stance I pinch myself hard, careful not to drop anything.

I'm still here.

I am ready.

Seeing my approach, Ethan pops up and grabs all three beers and the chips, transferring one of them to my now free hand with a little skip, and handing one to Rachel before plopping back into his lawn chair. He tears into the chips, the smile even bigger than I remember.

I'm too antsy to sit, and I kind of step back and forth nervously, taking in the gathering, Alice enthusiastically gabbing with some of Mom's friends on the porch, her husband over with a crowd of men around the grill. Mom's standing near the door now, wine in hand, a contented smile playing about her lips. Catching me looking, she winks. I offer the slightest nod.

Rachel and Ethan both left their girlfriends at home, implicitly understanding it had to be just the three of us. Everyone else seems to pick up on this too, or perhaps a choice few are practicing crowd control, but either way we're alone by the maple. It almost feels scripted, a moment built too big after too many years.

We sip our beers in silence. My heart skips a beat, suddenly certain this will be awkward, the moment gone, the impossibility proven! Desolation threatens to shatter hope, and the view from my tiny mountain home fills my mind's eye. Alone. Safe. A surge of emotion in the pit of my stomach brings me back, and I shake off the vision. I am safe! I *am* home.

I stop swaying nervously, noting the cool breeze ruffling my skirt. Slipping my shoes off, I curl my toes into the warmth of the grass and close my eyes, focusing on the goosebumps it sends up my legs. Sound closes off around me, like the cabin of an airplane pressurizing, and in this smallest of moments, time stops. I breathe it in, hold my breath for a few seconds, relish it. The fear passes.

Opening my eyes I find Ethan watching, biting his lip, and Rachel staring at my bare feet, sporting a bemused smile. Feeling my gaze she looks up, and once our eyes meet I know. We all feel it. Ethan mutters a quiet 'whew' into the silence and I'm instantly dizzy with the notion we've traveled back in time. We all share a snicker.

Rachel pipes up finally, raising her beer in a little toast, whispering. "Welcome home Suzy. Thanks for not dying."

The birds start chirping again with her interruption, followed quickly by the disjointed background noise of the party.

Ethan reaches over and clinks her bottle, looking up at me. "I'll second that, a hundred times over. Welcome home Suzy."

Placing the bottle between his knees, he does a little drum beat on his legs and the plastic armrests, "We are," thumpa, thump, "so glad," thumpa, thump, thump, thump, "You're here!" Clink! Smacking the bottle, then a dramatic finish blowing into it. Epic smile.

Curtsying twice, at them both individually, "No problem. Dying would have sucked." Sobering a little, I offer, "It was pretty terrifying actually, waking up with that tube in my throat and all, not knowing where I was."

Rachel raises both eyebrows, half smile in place. "Ethan, we should have tried another butterfly handjob, to save Suzy!"

Blushing, his mouth a straight line behind the lip of his bottle, he squints at her, "I wondered how long it would take you to toss that into play."

I'm laughing, "Oh? Do tell? What is this butterfly handjob you speak of?"

Rachel's trying not to laugh. "Ethan? Care to enlightening our dear friend Suzy?"

He straightens up, tilting his head to the left and raising his eyebrows, donning a patronizing look, "Well it seems, dear friend, that my M.O. in high school was making out with girls with whom romantic potential was zero. Furthermore, my magic penis had the effect of driving you away while simultaneously saving Rach from fucking that shit for brains guy, Steve."

She leans over and slaps him on the arm, sounding hard enough to hurt. "That's not what it saved me from, you jerk! It was sweet. Took our friendship to a whole new level." Pausing, she muses, "That thing is dangerous though. You really ought to be careful with it around your friends."

Chuckling, he taps his bottle with a pensive frown, "Makes you wonder what would happen if I let John have a turn."

A sudden rush of pleasure between my legs makes my knees weak. Taking a confused step forward I regain my balance, face flushed.

Rachel notes this, raising an eyebrow at me, but only offers, "He does have nice legs, you kinda want to chew on them a little."

Laughing, we cock our heads at her in unison.

She shrugs. "What? I can't appreciate a nice set of legs? Shit that's why I date soccer girls!"

Ethan leans towards her, fingers in a little steeple under his chin, then pointing at her gently. "You said something about another butterfly handjob, and now you're chewing on men's legs." Pauses a beat. "Should Josie be worried?"

She pushes his fingers aside, loudly declaring, "Ethan, the only penis for me is yours!" drawing a bark of a laugh from someone in the distance.

Crossing her legs, bouncing a foot, she mimes writing in an imaginary notepad, speaking slowly as she writes, "Dear Diary. If I ever need a penis, comma, Ethan!! Exclamation, exclamation." She smiles up at us briefly, then furrows her brow, going back to the notepad. "Gonna draw a little penis, heeere," pauses, making elaborate strokes, "Little hearts all around!" clucks once with her tongue, admiring her handiwork. Satisfied, she puts it into an imaginary breast pocket, pats her boob.

Ethan and I look at each other, then he turns back to her, mumbling through a sip of his beer, "You didn't have to make it a *little* penis."

Huffing, Rachel mimes whipping the notebook back out, tossing it over her shoulder, "Well I don't have any goddamn poster board Ethan!"

We exchange about three glances apiece, bouncing from face to face, Ethan smirking, Rachel's half smile threatening to explode. We're all holding out, waiting for Rachel's infectious laugh to entangle us all, but I don't make it!

The next thing I know I'm laughing so hard I can't breathe, on my knees trying not to spill my beer, an extra challenge with this damn cast. I fail, and actually collapse onto my side when I can't hold myself up with a beer in my only good hand. I lay there and shake, an uncontrollable, quivering mess of giggles!

Struggling back up, I shuffle on my knees over between the two lawn chairs and throw my arms around the best friends I can imagine! I accidentally clock Rachel on the head with my cast, drawing a grunt from her but escalating our belly laughs epically!

I try to shake it off, pursing my lips and blowing out in huffs, finally gasping, "Oh Rachel! Ethan! I love you both, I always have, I always will!"

Rachel's laugh crying turns to real crying and she hugs me close, then reaches across me to grab Ethan's neck. "Suzy, Ethan, I love you both, I always have, I always will."

Ethan doesn't say anything, but suddenly leans his chair heavily onto the both of us. At first I think he's overcome with emotion, and I try to support him. Too late I realize of course it's just Ethan being Ethan, and he shoves with his far foot, tumbling all three of us to the grass!

Untangling from the jumble of bodies and lawn chairs, we end up side by side, looking up at the clouds, giggling lightly.

Rachel's between us, lying on Ethan's arm, and she and I are holding hands. Instantly I'm transported back to that field by our old oak. Those epic nights when we camped under the stars, life an unfolding tapestry of adventure all around us, the world our own. I haven't felt that way in so long. Too long. I squeeze Rachel's hand, and she gives me a long squeeze back.

Quietly, Ethan whispers, "I love you both, I always have, I always will."

A breeze drifts through the nearby maple, a few leaves cascading our way. It's not the oak, but the change feels right. It feels perfect.

After a moment I jump up, shadow box the air for a moment, exclaiming, "There's one more wrong to right my friends!"

With purpose I stride over to the driveway, not surprised to find Jasper leaning against the Scout, always proudly on display at any function. One of his friends is there, who offers a polite 'welcome home' before ducking away.

Jasper crinkles his eyes at me lightly, the corners of his mouth offering a few twitches. Noting my determined stance, he says nothing.

I pat the Scout's hood, "Still runs?"

Now he smiles, running his hand along the doorframe, "Of course. Maybe we should take her out for ice cream later, so you can see."

I cock my head a little, raise an eyebrow, take a long draught of my beer. Pointing at my spot, "I dunno. Have you fixed the passenger door?"

His expression slides into Rachel's half smile, "You know, that door catch was never a hard fix."

I process this briefly, then decide we're speaking the same language. I stand up a little straighter and go for it.

"Jasper, you're the only father I've ever known. I want to call you daddy again."

He stares at me, but I can see his eyes are wet. A beat passes, then ever so softly, and betrayed by the slightest quiver in his lower lip, he says only, "I'd like that."

No big hug here. We toast beer bottles and take a swig together. He winks. I nod once and turn back to the party.

Halfway across the lawn, I pause, taking in Rachel and Ethan. He's sitting up slightly, leaning on both arms propped behind him, legs askew. His toothy smile absorbs his face. Rachel's nestled into his side, lips closed but eyes bright, the constant half smile ready to burst into infectious laughter at any moment. They might as well be nine years old again, under that old oak.

I hold both hands to my chest, cradling the cast and beer bottle against me. We stare at each other for a long moment, and I hold them there until I am full.

Slowly, gently, I begin to dance.

ACKNOWLEDGMENTS

I write with a soundtrack, so first I'd like to thank a few of the artists I had in heavy rotation. The Magnetic Fields, Bon Iver, Phosphorescent, Sufjan Stevens, TORRES, Joni Mitchell, Amen Dunes, John Maus, Kishi Bashi, Lambchop, London Grammar, Emmy the Great, Ben Howard, and Roo Panes, together you consistently set the mood, your lyrics inspired, and I couldn't have done it without you!

I want to thank the Big Five, who suffered in turn through twenty-five years of my emotional education. Leigh, Courtney, Gudrun, Heather and MB, you each offered your own, unique take on relationships and the meaning of human connection, immensely shaping my own search. I am forever grateful, and remember each of you fondly.

The inspiration for this novel wouldn't be complete without acknowledging my two heterosexual lifemates! Greg, who I grew up with, careful not to tumble out of his Scout's wonky passenger door, and Ryan, my roommate and adventure partner through most of our twenties, a Radford Manor legend.

A thank you to my mother, who didn't live to see this published but was ecstatic to hear about it, radiating pride from her bed. And my father, who always treated me like a little adult, then later a friend as he watched my migration from Finance to Nursing to living in a van with a bemused acceptance and respect.

To my Uncle Glenn, whose easy laugh and antics left me with big shoes to fill for my little nieces, Riley and Ellie, and to Jed and Angela for letting me try. Being Uncle Yeti continues to be an all new exploration in the realm of connection.

To Laurel, who holds my hand today, and bore the weight of being my sole reader for far too long. Thank you for your continued support while I agonized over editing, despite clutter and dishes piling up around me.

And a small digression, if I may. The highs and lows working in ICU gives you emotional whiplash. Being part of the well-oiled ICU team, saving a life against the odds, only for the next patient to crash and die amidst the controlled chaos. Tragic stories, bereft families, then the patient who visits from rehab, walking in on their own two feet despite their month in ICU.

Through it all, it is a privilege to care for another human being. Few have such a physically and emotionally intimate job, or the daily opportunity to touch someone's life, where adjusting a dying patient's pillow can be a monumental comfort. I want to thank all my patients for allowing me to be their nurse, and for everything I've learned about the human condition in the experience.

One patient in particular came to mind as I pondered what to say from this soapbox. A little old lady who was remarkable not just for being universally kind and thankful, but also for maintaining her sense of humor as her body gave up. I volunteered to be her nurse every shift, and she would tease me, smiling and trying to giggle as she huffed through shortness of breath. Weeks went by without improvement, and eventually she elected to stop all care, said her goodbyes without trepidation, and we kept her comfortable as she passed quietly.

Throughout her ICU stay she embodied the notion 'We can't change what happens to us, but we can do our best to choose how we react.' I want to thank her for the joie de vivre permeating her every action, right up to the end. Her attitude and easy connection with everyone made her a rare patient, the kind who gave us more than we gave her. She was a true inspiration.

Lastly, a special thanks to everyone who encouraged me

to write, an echo persisting across the years, whispered in an eerie unison by English teachers, professors, managers, employees, colleagues and friends.

Thank you all.

ABOUT THE AUTHOR

Seeking meaning, Eric abandoned a career in finance to work on an ambulance, later selling everything he owned to live in a van, tooling around the West while delving into the depths of human tragedy as a critical care nurse. His journey included four degrees, MS/BS Math, BS Nursing, and most interestingly, a BS in Psychology, focusing on human connection, gender relations, and sexuality.

An avid backpacker, he has spent months in the wilderness, covering thousands of miles over large chunks of the Appalachian Trail and Pacific Crest Trail, among numerous others. He has also explored the backcountry in Patagonia, Norway and Canada.

Tiring of full-time van life, he purchased a tiny cabin in the mountains, where most of this novel was written. Gazing at the view, with music shaping the vibe and a cup of coffee or tea in hand, he penned Susan's journey. Appropriately, this view became the novel's cover art.

He currently lives in an actual house, in Missoula, Montana, with his partner Laurel and her thirty-five-year-old stuffed raccoon. When he's not working at the local hospital, now as a nephrology nurse, he can be found trail running in the surrounding mountains. He is well known for his love of burritos.